back in th

geoffrey Willans
and ronald searle

Back
in the Jug
Agane

COLLINS
LIONS

First published 1959 by Max Parrish & Co Ltd, London
First published in this Lion edition 1973
by William Collins Sons & Co Ltd
14 St James's Place, London s w 1
Second Impression March 1974

Printed in Great Britain
by William Collins Sons & Co Ltd, Glasgow

CONTENTS

I MITE HAV KNOWN

Well i mite hav expected it. The game's up. They got me just when i thort i was safe. So here i am back at SKOOL agane for a joly term chiz chiz chiz.

St custard's, i regret to report, hav not changed in my absence, though perhaps it may hav got worse. It is just the same as any other first day since i started my akademic hem-hem career there some few semesters ago. (It seme as if it were yesterday, my dere). Same cobwebs, same smell of wet flannel, soap, carbolik ect poo gosh: inside the skool piano there is now a nest of mice, 1 cig. card, 3 katerpillers and pikture of marylyn monro pinched no doubt from the master's comon room.

As for my merry felow students, they are still here worse luck. Just look at them – grabber who arrive in a swank-pot rolls, peason my frend who hav a face like a squished tomato, gillibrand, molesworth 2 my bro. And who is this who skip weedily up to me, eh? 'Hullo clouds, hullo sky,' he sa. 'Hullo birds, hullo poetry books, hullo skool sossages, hullo molesworth 1.' You hav guessed it is dere little basil fotherington-tomas.

Wot brethless adventures lie before these stout little chaps? (And none stouter than fatpot peason.) Wot wizard japes and priceless pranks will they get up to? Before them lie the bright future of a new term – will they accept the chalenge?

(*Now read on.*)

On arrival all boys stand about with hands in pokets looking utterly fed up and dejected. Finally someone speke.

'Did you hav a good hols, molesworth?'

'Not bad.'

(*Silence.*)

'Did you gave a good hols peason?'

'Not bad.'

The dialogue is positively scintilating, my dere. Surely they canot kepe it up? There is no chance of that for the wit of these skolars is interupted by a dread sound e.g.

CLANG-PIP. CLANG-PIP. CLANG-PIP.

It is the skool bell which sumon us to asemble in big skool into which enter anon GRIMES, the headmaster surounded by a posse of thugs and strong-arm men in black gowns. The beaks, of course, alias 'my devoted staff'. You can imagine it a few minits before.

Scene: GRIMES study. A candle is burning in a botle. A botle of GIN stand on the table. A beak is fixing an iron spike on a kane, another is fixing a knuckle-duster, a third practise with a broken botle.

GRIMES: Are they all in, Slugsy?

G. A. POSTLETHEWAITE m.a. (leeds): Yep, they're all in, boss.

GRIMES: o.k. then we're ready to pull the job. You kno the plan. Slugsy, you cover me from the door. Lefty, cover my right flank. Butch, on the other side. Killer, bring up the rear, If there's any trouble, let them hav it. That clear Butch?

P. ST. J. NETLETON, b.a. (exeter): Wot about our cut? You still owe us for last terms jobs.

GRIMES: How can you be so sordid?

ect. ect. ect.

Now GRIMES stand on the platform, smiling horibly at the pitiable colection of oiks, snekes, cads, oafs and dirty roters below.

Before them lie the bright future of a new term – will they accept the chalenge?

'Welcome back,' he snarl, 'Welcom back to st. custards for a new term. I hope you had a good hols? i did myself – spane, the s. of france, then on for a couple of weeks to the italian riviera. This term, of course, the fees will be higher to meet the mounting costs.'

But this evidence of good humour is short-lived. Without warning, he bare his fangs.

'Now listen, scum,' he yell, 'The last mum hav departed in tears. You are in my clutches agane and there is no escape. And its going to be this way this term. More work, increased production, trades unions supresed and the first boy i hear who sa poo gosh at a skool sossage will get 6. And strikes won't help you. If you go out the shop stewards will be flogged.'

'Remember this,' he leer, 'You never had it so good.'

Well, this is just wot we expect. We hav it every term and our tiny harts sink to our boots. It will be nothing but *lat. fr. arith. geom. algy. geog.* ect. and with the winter coming on it would be warmer in siberia in a salt mine. Oh well – we wait for wot we kno will come next.

'And wot,' sa GRIMES, 'have we all been reading in the hols?'

Tremble tremble moan drone, i hav read nothing but red the redskin and Guide to the Pools. i hav also sat with my mouth open looking at lassie, wonder horse ect on t.v. How to escape? But i hav made a plan.

'fotherington-tomas,' sa GRIMES, 'wot hav you read?'

'Ivanhothe vicar of wakefieldwuthering heights treasureislandvanity fairwestwardhothewaterbabies and —'

'That is enuff. Good boy. And molesworth?'

He grin horibly.

'What hav you read, molesworth?'

gulp gulp a rat in a trap.

'Proust, sir.'

'Come gane?'

'Proust, sir. A grate fr. writer. The book in question was swan's way.'

'Gorblimey. Wot did you think of it, eh?'

'The style was exquisite, sir, and the characterisation superb. The long evocative passages—'

'SILENCE!' thunder GRIMES. 'There is no such book, impertinent boy. I shall hav to teach you culture the hard way. Report for the kane after prayers.'

Chiz chiz to think i hav learned all that by hart. It's not fair they get you every way. And so our first day end when we join together singing our own skool song.

> St. custard's is brave.
> SWISH.
> St. custard's is fair.
> BIFF BANG WALOP.
> Hurrah hurrah for st. custard's.
> SWISH SWISH SWISH.

As lashed by the beaks we join our boyish

trebles in this fine old song we feel positively inspired
i do not think. We are in for the joliest term on
record. In fakt, i am back in the jug agane.

THE GRIMES POLL

Headmaster GRIMES lay down his mitey pen. The
crossed skool nib hav ceased scratching: the watery
skool ink is dry upon the ex book: candle in the
bottle in his studdy gutter fitfully. 'Finished,' he sa.
'Completed.'

To wot do he refer, eh? Is it to the corektions of
our weedy lat prep i.e. balbum amas puellae? Could
it be, perhaps, a letter to our pore parents putting
up the fees? Could it be the anual statement of his
whelk stall accounts? No chiz it is none of these things.
It is his master work on the behaviour of boys –
SECRETS OF THE BOOT ROOM by phin-
eas GRIMES, b.a. (stoke-on-trent) to be published
in the autumn by messers grabber at 30 bob.

However by courtesy of the molesworth chizzery
and spy service it is now possible to reveal some of
the startling fakts contaned in this huge opus.

TELEVISION

Out of 62 pupils at st. custard's, $61\frac{1}{2}$ stay up late at
nite gawping at the t.v. To do this they employ
unbelievable cuning saing mum, can we? ect. o pleese,
mum, just till 7.30 when that grate dog who rescue
people and bark like mad will be finished. $61\frac{1}{2}$ mums

out of 62 fall for this becos it means a little quiet in the house (xcept for the grate dog barking, this, however, appere preferable to our boyish cries.) Wot hapen next? The grate dog is folowed by an even grater fool i.è. plunket of the yard. This is a program highly suitable for small boys as there is murder and various other CRIMES in it. The grate thing is to manage to sit gawping until the new program begin: then, when yore mum come in and sa britely 'Time for bed, chaps' ect, she will get wraped up in the brutal crime which go on. This take 61½ boys out of 62 until 8 p.m. when there is a quiz chiz. Pater storm in and sa 'aren't these boys in bed yet?' He then kno the answer to the first q. i.e. wot is the capital of england? This set him going since he wish to give a demonstration of his prowess.

'Any fule would kno that,' he sa.

61½ boys out of 62 restrane any comment on this, knoing they will get sent to bed. Pater go on saing weedy things i.e. china, of corse, edison, e.a.poe also that he ought to go in for it he would win a lot of money. mum do not restrane coment on the last point and by the time the argument is over we can have a little peace with the play. This is about LUV and of no interest but it do kepe you on the job until 10. The 61½ boys then get into there pajamas and come back to sa good nite. They stretch forward for loving embrace when sudenly they are turned into pilar of salt. e.g. lot's wife becos a HORSE is in terible trubble on the screen with a ruough master. 11 p.m. bed and swete dreams.

SMOKING

Enuff said. Just count the cig ends behind the skool potting shed. It look as if the skool gardner must smoke 500 a day.

CONVERSATION IN DORMS

The news is grave. 62 boys out of 62 indulge in this forbiden practise after lights out. Moreover the conversation is not on a high level i.e. you hav a face like a squished tomato same to you with no returns ass silly ass i said it first yes i did no i didn't. This frequently end up in BLOWS with ye olde concrete pilows. From 1 boy alone do we get GOOD CONVERSATION i think you kno to whom i refer. Oui! c'est basil fotherington- (hullo clouds, hullo sky) tomas who bore us to slepe with proust and t.s.eliot.

RUSHING DOWN THE PASSAGE

There is something about the sight of a passage which raise the worst in a boy. No sooner than he see the end of it than he wish to sa charge ta-ran-ta-rah and do so, sliding the soles off his house shoes. $\frac{1}{2}$ a boy, however, do walk slowly and with corekt deport-ment, one hand on hip, until overtaken and troden on by the mob. And good ridance.

MOB VIOLENCE

We must do something about this: we canot hav it, you kno. In future there must be no more scrums in the gim. The honor of the skool is at stake. And the answer is easy. Organise some morris dancing and all will be well. Or not.

And wot is GRIMES conklusion, eh? Modern youth is on the way down. But he was a boy once (i suppose). Can it get any lower?

MUSIC THE FOOD OF LUV

Sooner or later yore parents decide that they ought to give you a chance to hav a bash at the piano. So wot hapen, eh? They go up to GRIMES, head-master, who is dealing in his inimitable way, my dere, with a number of problems from other parents e.g. fotherington-tomas's vests, peasons cough drops, grabber's gold pen and pore, pore mrs gillibrand thinks that ian (who is so sensitive) is the tiniest bit unhappy about the condukt of sigismund the mad maths master. (Who wouldn't be? He is utterly bats and more crooked than the angle A.) Finally come the turn o those super, smashing and cultured family hem-hem the molesworths. Mum step forward britely:

Oh, mr GRIMES, she sa, we think it would be so

nice for nigel and his wee bro, molesworth 2, to learn the piano this term.

(GRIMES thinks: Another mug. One born every minit.)

GRIMES: Yes, yes, mrs molesworth, i think we could manage to squeeze them in. Judging from their drawings both yore sons hav strong artistick tendencies. i see them in their later years drawing solace from bach and beethoven ect in some cloistered drawing room. It'll cost you ten nicker and not a penny less.

PATER: (*feebly*) I sa—

GRIMES: Look at the wear and tear on the piano – it's a bektenstein, you kno. Then there's the metronome – had to have new sparking plugs last hols and the time is coming when we've got to hav a new pianoforte tutor.

Pater and Mater weakly agree and the old GRIMES cash register ring merily out again. It is in this way that that grate genius of the keyboard, molesworth 2, learned to pla that grate piece fairy bells chiz chiz chiz.

The first thing when you learn to pla the piano is to stare out of the window for 20 minits with yore mouth open. Then scratch yore head and carve yore name, adding it to the illustrious list already inscribed on the top of the piano. Should, however, GRIMES or any of the other beaks becom aware that there is no sound of mery musick, the pupil should pretend to be studdying the KEYBOARD

Before getting on to rimski-korsakov it is as well to kno wot
you are up aganst

in his instruktion book.

This is meant to teach the eager pupil the names
of the notes ect. The skool piano may hav looked like
that once, but toda it is very different. Before getting
on to rimski-korsakov it is as well yo kno wot you
are up aganst. Here is the guide –

C—this one go plunk.

D—the top hav come off the note and you strike
melody from something like a cheese finger.

E—sticks down when you hit it. Bring yore
screwdriver to lever it up.

F—have never been the same since molesworth
2 put his chewing gum under it.

G—nothing hapen when you hit this note at all.

Do not be discouraged, however, show grit, courage, determination, concentrate, attend and soon you will get yoreself a piece. This will probably be called Happy Thorts and there is a strong warning at the beginning which sa Not Too Fast. Who do they think i am, eh, stirling moss?

Scene: fort twirp, h.q. of davy croket, wyatt earp, last of the mohicans, lone ranger ect. Enter a quaver spuring his horse.

QUAVER: (*quavering*) Larrfffing lemonade, the Indian semi-breve is on the war path.

CROKET: Oo, gosh!

EARP: This is yore job, lone ranger, i guess.

L RANGER: Wouldn't want to get mixed up with all them breves and semi-breves, mr earp. To sa nothing of the crotchets and quavers. When they get mad, they get real mad. Where's the sheriff?

(*Enter Chief Larrfffing Lemonade*).

CHIEF L L.: i feel really crotchety. Guess i'll have a half of minim . . .

Ect. And so it go on. But wot really hapen, when yore aged musick mistress is on the job?

'And a one, to, three . . . softly, softly, molesworth, that is a pedal not a clutch . . . and a two, three, four . . . lah-dee, dah . . . this is a lake not an ocean . . . get cracking . . . hep, hep . . . sweetly, sweetly . . . hit the right note, rat.'

Well, musick is just another of those things. Wot i sa is. Either you have it or you haven't. And i would rather not.

'Wot is yore opinion of colin wilson, the new philosopher?' sa fotherington-tomas, hanging by his weedy heels from the cross bar.

'Advanced, forthright, significant,' i repli, kicking off the mud from my footer boots.

'He takes, i think, the place of t.s.eliot in speaking for the younger genneration. Have you any idea of the score?'

'Not a clue.'

'Those rufians hav interrupted us 6 times. So one must assume half a dozen goles. If only our defence was more lively, quicker on the takle! Now as i was saing about colin wilson –'

Yes, clots, weeds, and fellow suferers, it means the good old footer season is with us and jack the shepherd is a good deal warmer when he blows his nail then we are. Birds are frozen: little children sink with a vast buble in the mud and are not heard of agane: sigismund the mad maths master don his long white woollen hem-hems. Yes, this is the time when we are driven out with whip and lash upon ye old soccer field.

Mind you, there are some who think soccer is super. These are the ones who charge, biff, tackle and slam the leather first-time into the net ect. They hav badges and hav a horible foto taken at the end of term with their arms folded and the year chalked upon the pill. This foto cost there parents 7/6 on the skool bill and i hope they think it is worth it. i would not care for grabber's face on my walls, that's all.

Of corse i'm no good . . . no, i mean it . . . i simply am no good . . . no, please, grabber, my body-swerve . . . well, it go in the wrong direcktion . . . o, i sa, no . . . wot a nice thing to hear about myself . . . if i try hard i'll be in *the seconds!* And then how much further on would i be in the career of life, eh?

I speke for millions when i sa i *AM NO GOOD AT SOCCER.* You can, of corse, watch it from the touchline in that case. Very diffrent.

'Pass . . . get it out to the wing . . . move in to the centre . . . wot are you plaing about at? . . . Get rid of it.'

I need hardly tell you the esential thing about a football i.e. nobody need tell *me* to get rid of it. i do not want it in the first place. Wot is the use of having a soaking wet piece of leather pushed at you? Give me a hadock every time, at least you can eat it.

However, where would headmaster GRIMES be without the good old game? No longer would he be able to look up from those delicious crumpets, which he eat before a roring fire and observe: 'The third game ort to be finished in about 20 minits. Cold out there. About 50 below zero. Damn it, forgot to stoke the baths! o well, a spot of cold water did nobody any harm, eh?'

However, there is no doubt about it the honour of the old skool depend a grate deal on whether you can score more than wot i may litely call 'the oposi-tion'. Scoring more than the 'oposition' is practically imposible, but it sometimes hapen. Beware when it

'Mind you, there are som who
think soccer is super.'

do becos you hav to bang yore spoon on the table,
just when you want to help yourself to the jam,
and yell RA, RA, RA! Well done SKOOL
SKOOL, SKOOL!

And who is it who have achieved this sukcess?
None other than the games master, who hav given
his life, his time, his bootlaces and his premium
bonds into making the 1st XI into a well-oiled
footballing machine. There are lots of diffrent kinds
of games masters, but there are usually 2 types who
are able to be distinguished by us weeds on the
touchline e.g.

Type One: He do no not sa anything: he put his
hands in his mack and watch. After about 17 minits
of the first half he is heard to sa 'O, potts-rogers'. He
knock out his pipe at half-time when the team are
sucking lemons and whisper: 'good show, get on

with it.' Then he relapse into silence and, about 2 minits from time, sa 'o god'.

The other type of games master is exactly the oposite. Remembering his own football prime (one day we must go into the rekords of games masters, must we not?) he think he can score a gole with his own voice. Some of them can: or ort to be able to.

'COME ON, ST. CUSTARD'S . . . GET INTO HIM . . . PASS! . . . MARK YORE MAN! . . . BLOW YORE NOSE . . . INTO THE CENTRE. . . . NO, THE CENTRE NOT THE ARTERIAL ROAD . . . GET IT IN! . . . COME ON NOW! SHOOT! . . .'

This is the last desparing cry. Lots of games masters have been carted awa murmuring faintly 'Shoot!' In 999 cases if they were aiming at gole someone missed: but ocasionaly the shot hit the mark. And it was an elfin-ray pistol with atommic atachment that do the damage.

A TEACHER'S WORLD

'The New Year stretches before us, molesworth,' sa fotherington-tomas, skipping weedily.

'Wot of it?' i sa 'Wot of it, o weedy wet? It will be the same as any other, all geom.fr. geog ect and weedy walks on sunda.'

'It was just – well, have you ever thort of becoming a skoolmaster when you grow up?'

Curses! Curses! That i should live to see the day when these things were spoken!

'Sa that agane,' i grit, 'and i will conk you on the head and/or thoroughly bash you up.'

'Do not,' he sa, 'get into a bate. i was only trying to help. A skoolmaster is better than a fashion designer. Besides, you hav all the qualifications.'

'Hav i?' i sa, in spite of myself. 'How super, fotherington-tomas. Tell me about them, go on o you mite.'

'You are qualified,' sa fotherington-tomas, 'becos you can frankly never pass an exam and have o branes. Obviously you will be a skoolmaster – there is no other choice.'

Enraged i buzz a conker at him. It miss and strike the skool dog wandsworth who zoom across the footer field at mach. 1 and trip the reff cheers cheers.

As it hapen this witty conversation take place during the 2nd XI footer match v porridge court. There comes a warning shout from the spektators. fotherington-tomas skip back weedily into gole and i remane where i am, a bleeding hart on the left wing.

All the same the conversation have me worried and affekt my game. (See report)

> 'For the rest of the match molesworth 1 was not in the smashing form which have earned him the soobriquet of the "Dribbling Wizard." He was not fastening on to his passes.' (m. thinks: you mean when someone hack a huge muddy ball in my direction? Wot a pass.)
> 'The opposition had him at sea.' (m. thinks: it's amateurs still at prep skool, isn't it? Or are

porridge court buying players?) *'Where was that body swerve? That familiar jink?'* (m. thinks: Gone, my dear. Absolument disparu like mother's mink.)

And so it is the old story. The better team won, ha-ha. All clap each other on the back and hug each other. 'Where are your lovely flowers, molesworth, which porridge court spartak hav given you?' 'i hav thrown them to ye olde matronne before disappearing into the dressing room.' Well you kno wot go on in there. WAM BIFF SOCKO ZOOSH. CRASH. BASH. Headmaster GRIMES emerge smiling. 'A little disappointing but we must learn to swallow defeat.'

'Of corse,' sa mater. 'How are nigel's spots?'

'Hav he got spots? gosh chiz i haven't had measles yet myself. i must get awa from this.'

'I was a little *surprised* to find him playing. nigel is so delikate, so thin, so nervy, so tense, so neurotick (strike out the word which do not apply). i felt that he mite perhaps hav been in bed ect. . . .'

And so it go on at football matches. But, as that nite i lie awake on my downy couch hem-hem in the PINK DORM the conversation come back to me as it was a nightmare. Me a Skoolmaster! Me a BEAK! Me an Usher! Wot an idea – and yet look around you. There are so many of them that it is obviously a fate which is difficult to avoid.

My head nods the tired brane drowses. i slip i slide (peotry THE BROOK) into merciful oblivion. Soon the dorm resound with a steady note plaster falls off the ceiling, the paint blisters pop. My snores join the others but there is no rest i am shaken by a terible NIGHTMARE.

i am sitting at the master's desk looking with horor at a see of faces, fat ones, thin ones, contorted, spotty, green, and black ones, there is no doubt of whose they are – it is 3B.

And who is that horid creature dodging behind gillibrand and trying to conceal the fact that he is chewing buble gum? It is me, molesworth 1 chiz chiz chiz. *i am teaching myself!*

'Boy!' i rasp, in a voice i can scarcely recognise it is hoarse and thick with pasion. 'Boy, stand up. Wot is yore name?'

'molesworth 1, sir.'

'That is very interesting, molesworth very interesting indeed. Can it be, however, that you are having some difikulty in enunciating? i thort there was some slight suspicion of er congestion in the mouth? Some er impediment of the speech?'

'N—no, sir. Nnnnnnn—no, sir.'

'BOY HOW DARE YOU?'

My face is red as a tomato i shake with rage my eyes are those of a MANIAK. Like any other master i hav forgotten that i was ever a boy i have forgoten brave noble fearless youth cheers cheers. My hand go back like a flash and i buzz the red chalk striking the victim on the nose. The rest of the klass titter they are sicophants and toadies i diskard them.

'If there is another sound i shall keep the whole

klass in. Molesworth, go outside and remove that disgusting objekt.'

It is too horible. i struggle to awake but the nightmare continue.

It is still the same lesson and i am the master. Everything is normal i am feeling a trifle lazy and set the boys some geom propositions to get on with. Before me is a pile of uncorekted exercise books i pop outside for a quick cig and return to study a book on grips and tortures for boys. i am immersed in this when i hear a sound.

'Sir,'

(A spasm of anoyance run through my frame. i pretend not to hear.)

'Sir, sir, sir please sir.'

CURSES! Is the child not to be put off? am i never to be rid of his importunity? Wearily i raise my bespectakled face and gaze at him over a mountane of exercise books and bottles of red ink.

'Well, wot is it molesworth?'

'Wot is the verb-noun infinitiv, sir?'

'Eh?'

'The verb-noun infinitiv, sir. It sa in the Shorter Latin Primer . . .'

'All right all right. i heard you the fust time' (thinks: verb-noun infinitiv? i dunno. search me.)

Open lat. grammer under cover of books. shufle shufle. Sweat pour from my brows i must play for time. i cover my action with stinging words.

'So molesworth you do not kno the verb-noun infinitiv? Wot crassness, wot ignorance ect . . .'

Masters ushally keep their cribs and answer books in the dark depths of their desks and wot a collection there is in there – kanes, beetles, chalk, thumbscrews,

It is me, molesworth 1 chiz chiz chiz i am teaching myself.

old tin soldiers which hav been confiskated, fotos of gurls, bat oil, fleas and cobwebs.

in here i find the lat. grammer. i prop it against a tin of pineaple chunks and find the answer. My blak beak's heart is filled with relief. Also i thirst for revenge. i switch to geom and make the chalk squeak with the compass on the blakboard until all howl

27

it is worse than molesworth 2's space ship.

SCREE SCREE SCREE SCREE delicious torture! i draw a collossal Angle A and make it equal to Angle B. Gloat Gloat. Wot does it matter if it is half the size? pythagoras could make an elephant equal to a flea . . .

Restlessly i toss from side to side in my bed. Can it be that i have eaten too much skool cheese? Why can i not awake? The nightmare continue . . .

am i popular? Do the boys like me? O grief. perhaps they do not. i will do anything. tomow i will read to them. i will give them the water babies that always sla them. it sla me too. Poor tom. And yet . . . are they making enuff progress? perhaps it should be the confidential clerk by t.s. eliot. But will that make me popular hem-hem?

THE BELL! The BELL!

I am telling a story about how i won the war. WEEE PING EEEAUOOWOO. Men, there is a nest of pea shooters under the map of that world i want you to silence them. CHARGE TA-RAN-TA-RA. BANG BONK BISH. Who zoom past then? it is molesworth 2 beating us up in his super-jet speed hawk ur ur ur ur. Take cover, Sigismund, these boys are fiercer than the mau-mau and many look like them. This is rebelion and the boys mean business. Give me my kane i will die like a man.

THE BELL.

Why have not mrs grabber given me the ushual 50 cigs for an xmas box? Where are my yelow socks and pink tie? i am alone the skool is empty. Where are the boys? Gone. it is the old story, caruthers, too many masters chasing too few boys. To many . . .

THE BELL.

And this time it is the skool bell bidding me rise and face the chalenge of the new year hem-hem, Sun shine, birds sing, skool sossages frazzle in the kitchen – hurrah hurrah i am not a master after all. I stride forth with new knoledge e.g. even masters hav their problems. i will remember that in future.

MOLESWORTH WOT ARE YOU DOING WITH YORE HAIR UN-BRUSHED YORE SHOES UNLACED AND WEARING ONE FOOTER SOCK ECT? DO 100000000000 LINES.

So you see. There you are. There's nothing you can do about them.

2

HURRAH FOR EXAMMS

Do examms hav any teror for you, clots? Are the
11-plus, G.C.E., common entrance ect preying on
your tiny mind? Are you posessed with a feeling that
you may fale? HAV YOU NOT WORKED
HARD ENUFF IN THE PAST, EH? Perhaps
you may not enjoy a briliant future as an atommic
physisist?

It is strange that i, molesworth, the goriller of 3B,
do not share these fears with you. Observe with what
confidence i stride into the examm room with new
sharpened old h.b., bungy, ruler and a stop watch
on ye olde chippendale desk. And wot then? I take
off my coat, roll up my sleeves and fold my stout
arms awaiting the q's with impatience. Not for me
the worried frowns of les autres, those careworn
looks. When the Beak bring round those papers
which smell so swetely of printer's ink this is wot
i sa:

Q.1. Complete the following series TR. S.G.P.
ME: Potty!

Q.2. Write the nex 3 numbers in this sequence:
1. 79. 232. 6 billion.

ME: Larrfably easy!

Q.3 A stupid old man walked 6 paces to the east, 12 to the north, stood on his head, then ran 100 yards at 100 m.p.h. Where is he?

ME: Too simple for words!

And so it go on. Of corse, criticks may point out that i occupy the lowly position of 9th out of 9 in 3B and am in some danger of relegation to div. 3. Why dost thou always put the obj in the nom, clot, aussi? Alas i canot deny the truth of these harsh words. Wot, then, is the sekrett of my sucksess in examms?

Hist, cave, come close felow skolars and suferers of the world of space and listen with all thy mitey ears, which, no doubt, hav not seen a towel for years.

My sucksess is not due to any stroke of good fortune but to careful planning in the past in association with my grate chum and felow research worker hem-hem wet peason. The results of our activities can now be anounced to the world i.e.

1. The molesworth/peason electronick brane which is disguised as a stop-watch. This amazing gadget can answer the most difficult question in a matter of secs enabling the skolar to sit back after 5 minutes with a look we kno so well in others which sa, 'That's pappy ect.' Any fule can use it and no beak will suspeckt.

2. The molesworth/peason portable roving eye. This is an intrikkate system of mirrors which can be flicked out of the poket (along with fluff, beetles, old

The molesworth/peason por

eye hav one serious defeckt.

cig. ends, stamp swaps ect) when the Beak is not looking and, in the space of $\frac{1}{8}$ secs can obtane the answers from all the other candidate's papers. The portable roving eye hav one serious operational defeckt, however. It hav been known to get 15 different reports, all of which sa *Puellam amas puer*, which, for some reason always get a cross aganst it and o marks.

3. Another triumph of science is the new molesworth/peason very high frequency radio set so that all boys can talk to each other on a wave length so high that no Beak can hear i.e.

CALLING BADGER ONE, CALLING BADGER ONE. HOW DO YOU HEAR ME, EH?

THY SWETE VOICE IS LOUD AND CLEAR, NIT-WIT WOT CAN I DO FOR YOU?

CALLING BADGER ONE. WOT IS THE ANSWER TO NUMBER THREE?

X TO THE POWER OF A OVER BETA, CLOT, AS ANY FULE KNO. WOT DO YOU MAKE OF NUMBER ONE?

NOTHING.

SAME HERE WE HAD BETTER CALL

UP FOTHERINGTON-TOMAS WHO ALWAYS KNO.

O.K. BADGER ONE. OUT.

So, by a carefull system of cross-checking each boy in the examm can get exactly the same answers.

Two further inventions upon which me and my emminent colleague are working are a magnifying glass for thumbnale cribs and a pill which send the Beak off to slepe. So why be worried, restless and iritable as examms approche? Give your mater and pater the poor skoolmasters confidence by yore calm attitude. These epoch-making products are on the market now, so send for catalog at once.

KO-EDDUKATION AT ST. CUSTARD'S

Hay ho! Wot a lot of problems we dere little chaps of the 20th century hav to face – there are H-bombs, missiles, spacemen, russians, yanks, electronick branes, headmasters, apart from the weedy ones in the arith books. Now as if these various chizzes are not enuff there is another i.e. i rede that in the society of the future there will be no such thing as boys skools and gurls skools. This can only mean ko-eddukation and already there are millions and trilions of brave noble and fearless boys who are being submitted to this fearful torture chiz chiz.

IT IS TIME THE SKANDAL WAS EXPOSED!

It is easy to immagine wot hapen at these ko-eddukational skools and we must rite it down fearlessly.

It is time the people knew. Pause while this scruffy scribe draw the CURTAIN aside.

Scene: a klassroom. This is much as ushual with blotch in the inkwells, ice cold radiator, railways carved on the desk, portrate of ceasar crossing the rubkon (1896), bits of aple core and beak's desk bulging with artikles which he hav confiskated. A klass is in progress with all the boys gazing out of windows with their mouths open and all the GURLS looking intent, eager, keen ect.

THE BEAK: molesworth, wot is the first rool of the 4 concords in lat.

(*No repli.*)

THE BEAK: MOLESWORTH!

ME: eh? Were you perchance adressing me sir?

THE BEAK (*with a vane effort at control*) i was asking you the first rool of the 4 concords, rat.

ME: Cor, stone the crows, search me!

THE BEAK: Perhaps some other boy will oblige
with the answer – peason, gillibrand, fotherington-
tomas? Is any boy reddy with an answer?
(*Silence meanwhile the gurls giggle and go mad with
xcitement. Finally, the beak turn his beetling brow to them
and his xpression become sudenly soft, his stern eye mild*)
'Mavis,' he whisper, 'perhaps you——?'

MAVIS: The first of the 4 rools of concord in lat is
that a Verb agrees with its subjekt in number and
person.
THE BEAK: Excellent, mavis!
MAVIS: Xamples are tempus fugit. Time flies.
THE BEAK: Bravo, now—
MAVIS: Or Libri leguntur. Books are read.
THE BEAK: Thank you, mavis, thank you.
MAVIS: (*continuing, nothing can stop her*) The second
rool of concord is that an adj or participle agree in
gender, number and case with the substantive it
qualify. Xamples – Vir bonus bonam uxorem
habet. The good man has a good wife.
ME: A highly debatable statement, if I may sa so, sir.

We get a bit of a larff for this but the day is lost
and mavis continue to the bitter end. And she is only
one becos ermintrude, matilda, mary and peggy are
all branes of britain, junior quiz champions ect.

Another thing GURLS have difrent standards of
behaviour in Klass i.e. if i thro a bit of bungy at
peason he will bide his time and thro an ink bomb
back which hit me splosh on the nose. But wot

hapen if you pull mavis pigtail, eh? You get a speech like this;—

MAVIS: I feel it my duty, sir, to report a trifling incident which hav just taken place. I feel that it will be for the good of the klass as a whole that i should do so. (Cries of 'sneke,' 'sneke') i am not alarmed by doing wot i conceive to be my duty. (*loud cheers and interjecktions of 'sit down,' 'sit down'*) Sir, these vulgar cries do not dismay me – nay (A member: 'Back her for the Derby') nay, nay (The price is slipping, six to four the field). This klass, sir, hav always had a reputation for clene living, decency, deckorum, and the preservation of behaviour-standards as recomended in the last phamplet by the min. of edukation obbtainable at the h.h. stionnery office, price 3 gns.

Wot (sa Mavis) Wot is the result?

A vulgarian whom i do not wish to name (Cries of name him, molesworth, who were you with last nite ect) A vulgarian whom I feel should be brought to book hav now sullied the honor of this mixed klass and brought to o the good name of the skool. By doing wot? He have pulled my pigtail.

Ow! (Once agane the molesworth touch bringeth ressults) *OW! OW! OW!*

And now i am glad to sa that mavis turn and swing with a short uppercut, following with a rite cross to the jaw. Human at last! She is once more champion of the world.

GURLS hav difrent standards of behaviour in Klass.

Well, there you are. Does ko-edducation work? Who will pla tag with me in the break, eh? Many people point to America and Russia and sa they hav had gurls and boys at skool together there for years. Does that make it any better? We venture hem-hem to think not. Hurrah for st custard's!

TENIS ANEBODY?

'Hullo, clouds, Hullo sky,' sa fotherington-tomas, skipping weedily by. 'Who's for tenis?'

i frown with anger, for i am looking at ye olde television chiz and robin hood is in a v. tuough spot indeed i.e. the sherif of nottingham is about to torture him with red hot irons, which is something we little tots are very used to. Anyway, i sometimes hav a feeling of sympathy for the sherif of notingham wot am i saing? Outside, of corse, it is a briliant, fine sumer day with bees buzzing, birds twittering ect.

'Who's for tenis?' repete fortherington-tomas, waving his racket.

'Go away, clot, You are standing in front of the screne. i can only hear the grones of agony.'

'Go on, molesworth, o you mite.'

'If i want tenis i can see it on the television,' i repli. 'Besides, it is a game for gurls.'

This is a new thing for the galant boys of the younger generration, they are always being told to pla tenis. Why is this? It is worse than criket becos at criket you can at least get bowled out but at tenis you hav to go on missing agane and agane and agane. i mean i expect it is all right if you can pla like those fierce people at wimbledon who go, well, you kno.

PUNG! PING! PING! PING! *PUNG!* HURRAH!

If i pla there is dead silence becos i never hit the pill at all they are all air shots chiz. Besides, am i likely to play a game at which fotherington-tomas can beat me, eh? i hav some pride.

Acktually fotherington-tomas is super at tenis, as he hav been coached by a pro at home i.e. he twiddle his raket and sa 'ruff or smooth?' and when he win he consider the direction of the wind, position of sun, met. forecast for next twenty-four hours, trend on the stock xchange, his horoscope for the week and sa finaly, 'i shall pla aganst the kool shade of the aple trees.' This mene that i am blinded by the sun and can only see fotherington-tomas crouched like a tiger on the other side of the net. Gosh, it take a bit for him to look like that it is strange wot a tenis raket can do.

It is strange wot a tenis raket can do.

If i get a pill over at all he wam it back at 90 m.p.h. so there is not much of a game at all.

Gurls, of corse, pla a lot of tenis at skool so i expect this explane the matter.

You kno wot hapen at gurl's skools they always discover a gurl who is the uggly duckling who can get into the skool six when pritty antonia trumpington brake her leg. Need i add that the olde skool de mademoisells always win the match?

'O, you juggins,' sa miss trent, the games mistress, crossly. Mavis bit her lip and faced the next ball with determination written all over her freckled face. Miss trent's powerful serve came into action agane but this time mavis faced it calmly and swept the pill into the far corner. On the next serve it hapened agane, then agane. 'Bravo, mavis,' cry miss trent. 'Well plaed, sir!' ect.

Personally i think in reel life miss trent would

41

probably be furious if any gurl swept her best serve into the far corner but that do not seme to hapen in books. Insted, miss trent put mavis in the tenis six and due to her briliant pla ect well, you kno.

Now that they hav pro tenis, in fakt, it would be a joly good wheeze if mavis and fotherington-tomas plaed a world tenis circus. Everyone would be agog when the skore stood at 499 matches each. Which will win the decider? Over to humphrey, the wet, in the commentator's box.

'mavis is serving. She hav thrown up the pill. It is still going up, up, up. Now it is in orbit. No, it is coming down. Plunk! Wot's this? O, ha-ha, *v. funny i must sa. It landed on mavis head. They're picking her up now. Second serve and the ball is up. Lovely style, mavis has. Now it's coming down. Oh dear, dear me, that is bad luck. It hav landed on mavis head agane.*

GAME TO FOTHERINGTON-TOMAS.

fotherington-tomas to serve and he is standing on the tips of his toes. He semes fascinated by clouds and sky. Bends to pick up the ball. Goodness gracious, how unfortunate. He hav split his trousis. He is covered in confusion and that is all. But who is this uncooth skoolboy who is roaring with larfter at the poor little chap's plight? Who can it be?

i give you 1 guess it is me, molesworth, the goriller of 3 B, delited at the fate of ickle pritty fotherington-tomas. It is a hard life to be a tenis star and, if mavis is an xample, you need a thick head which make me wonder why i am no good at the game. Oh well, back to the telly i must have mised 2 murders, 3 suicides

and a few loonies. Still, we'll be getting them
tomorrow.

MIND MY BIKE!

Well i mean to sa gosh chiz wot next, eh? Wot next?
Sitting in the old skool bibliotheque among the
cobwebs and reading the newspaper as is my wont
my eye leave the strip-cartoon and i see a headline.
'TESTS FOR CHILD CYCLISTS,' it sa.

'GAD!' i exclame, crumpling the paper into a ball
and buzzing it at ye old mappe of the world which
adorn the walls. 'GAD!'

Peason look up from the chair where he hav been
drawing beetles on his knee.

'Don't you kno there is a Silence Rool in the lib,
molesworth?'

'There is also a rool aganst chucking books, aganst
building forts out of the colekted works of lord
macaulay, aganst shooting peas at the bust of w.
shakespeare. Probably there is a rool against drawing
beetles on the knee also, thou weedy wet.'

'So wot, clot?' he retort, litely.

'Clearly you do not realise the importance of wot
hav taken place. They are going to test child cyclists.
They are going to give us weedy little badges if we
pass and if we fale – you will never guess, peason. i
canot bring myself to tell you.'

'Go on, molesworth, o you mite.'

'L-Plates,' i whisper.

Small wonder that peason grow pale benethe wot is his tan (i hope) Do not get me wrong, brothers and sisters, I am all for Road Safety ect becos it seme to me that the roads are v. dangerous places, especially when you see how GRIMES (headmaster) and SIGISMUND THE MAD MATHS MASTER drive their cranky old grids. But TESTS for veterans like me who have been awheel since my first fairy cycle at the age of 4! Curses! I know wot it will mean it will only be something more for me to fale becos the only thing i hav ever passed is molesworth 2 on his bike at mach. 1.

Wot with this and the 11 plus it seme that brave noble and fearless children are never going to be left alone until they become fearless metallurgists, clump press minders ect. You can imagine how it all happened.

Time: 1839.

Scene: the headmaster's studdy at No. 10 Downing Street. A kabinet meeting is in progress and GRIMES the prime minister is in the chair – altho i do not hardly think you could have expekted him to be sitting on the floor.

GRIMES: There's one more thing, gents, and strate i don't kno wot we're going to do about it. A scotish blacksmith called kirkpatrick macmillan hav invented a thing he call a bicycle.

THE MINISTER OF AGRICULTURE AND FISHERIES: Gosh!

GRIMES: Two wheels joined together with a bar and a saddle on top. Wheels within wheels ha-ha!

ALL: That's joly funny, sir. Ha-Ha!

GRIMES: Wheel, wheel, I'm glad you think so!

ALL: That's funy, too ha-ha-ha-ha-ha!

GRIMES: He must be a wheel proper inventer.

ALL: Stop it, sir, you're killing us!

GRIMES: All's wheel!

(*The Ministers disolve into fits of faned larffter. GRIMES strike the table with his kane.*)

GRIMES: That's enuff. It's not as funy as all that. The point is – wot are we going to do about it?

THE MINISTER OF TRANSPORT: We must hav action!

ALL (*thundering*): Action! Action!

GRIMES: Wot action are we to take?

THE MINISTER OF TRANSPORT: There's only one thing. We must set up a working party to report on the problem.

ALL: He's got it!

The P.M. get up, and shake him warmly by the hand: a

The future of the BICYCLE is still at stake.

decanter of port bursts like an H-Bomb, 6 topp hats sale into the air, the fr hav had it, the Gauls are at the gates of rome, wellington hav got his boots off, all's well with the world.

THE MINISTER OF AGRICULTURE AND FISHERIES: *(chortling):* Wheel, wheel! That's really v. witty. Wheel, wheel!

We pass now from this unsavoury episode from the hist. books (and how many, let's face it, there are, how many) to the present day. This is the age of elektronick branes, of diesel-electrick locos, of atommick power stations ect, ect: all these added to the ink darts, kanes, lat. grammers, headmasters, boys and beasts which have been going for a long time. Wot hav been going on in the meantime? The working party is still on the job and the future of the BICYCLE is still at stake. Now, indeed, it is more at stake than ever for they have come to consider the report on st. custard's, my dere old skool hurrah hurrah hem-hem. Here is the report:

C 3342 MG (357. st. custard's. Behaviour of skolars and tiny tots on bicycles.

Our spies hid in the bushes for weeks and were really upset by the spiders which did their best to hinder their observations. (We refer to the spies observations, not the spiders.) Wot our spies did observe was disstressing, i.e.

(a) One youth with pink bike, underslung handlebars, crash helmet, waterbotle, speedo, full tool kits detachable wheels ect ect. He appered to be known as grabber, head of the skool, wet, weed, sneke, monkey-face. owing to the strukture of his machine this youth rode with his nose near the ground and his hem-hem in conjunktion with the planet jupiter. he semed to hav contempt for those around him. We recomend L-Plates.

(b) A small boy of elfin appearance who employed a fairy cycle. His golden locks streamed in the breeze and he kept saing 'Hello clouds! Hullo, sky!' *L-Plate recommended.*

(c) molesworth 2 who zoom about on his bicycle with nose on the handlebars at 90 m.p.h. When questioned he repli that he is the last of the manned fighters and hav just brought down a guided missile.

(d) But who is this brave, staunch fellow who hav just finished oiling his machine? He mount, he ride steadily, he look left, right, left ect., he sound his bell, he is the pikture of quiet control. Who is it, eh? It is me, molesworth 1.

Well, there you are chiz. It isn't a state of affairs I am looking forward to but i supose if we had all ridden our bikes better in the past we shouldn't hav to go through all this now. If we all behave ourselves and do not zoom down hills they may set up another working party to consider whether fairy badges and L-Plates are not bosh and worth o. That at least is something to work for. Honk, honk, tinkle-tinkle and ho, for the wide open road. *WITH YORE EYES OPEN.*

Fr. and english are divided by more than the chanel.

FR. AND ENGLISH

You kno the trubble with paters and maters chiz, and particularly maters is that they are always trying to improve their dere little chicks. Hence the numerous corektions which we all kno at home i.e. you hav to hold yore knife properly, not make treakle pools in prodige, get clene hankerchiefs and take off yore hat to mrs jenkins ect. If you do all these things you will grow up to be as good a man as yore pater tho this statement makes your mater look a bit thortful.

Behold, then, the scene at ye olde molesworth brekfast table when there come the cheerful rat-tat of the postman's knock.

'That's the postman,' sa the molesworths all together, for they are a brilliant family and full of branes hem-hem.

'Go and get the letters, nigel dere.'

'Wot me? Me? Why shouldn't molesworth 2 get them i got them the last time did didn't did ect.' (We don't kno why children go on like that but they do i am afrade.)

Eventually after this unsemely debate of which we ort to be thoroughly ashamed i do not think the letters arive at the table amongst the swete smell of korn flakes, marmalade ect.

'Ah!' sa yore mater. 'Here it is.'

She hold aloft a weedy letter written in purple ink with a fr. stamp which is not worth a d. as a swop.

'Armand is coming to sta with us in the hols,' she sa.

'Who, pray, is armand,' i repli, dealing a mitey blow to my hard-boiled egg. 'As far as i kno he is the weedy wet in the fr. book who sa the elephants are pigs.'

'He is a fr. boy who is coming to us to learn eng.,' sa mater with a swete patient smile. 'And you arc to be v. nice to him as the pore boy will be far from home ect.'

Well, you can imagine wot any noble british boy would sa to that i.e. o *no*, mater, must we, gosh, wot a chiz ect. but it is no use. It is not any good pointing out that 'chez molesworth' he may learn a lot o things but one of them won't be eng. We kno when we are licked.

Interval of 3 weeks. Then ARMAND arive you

can well immagine him only he is worse than anything you can immagine.

Armand is 6 ft tall, wear short pants, and look upon molesworth 2 et moi as if we were a pare of shoppkeepers (c.f. napoleon in the hist. books). The trubble is he can speke eng.

'So ziz is yore owse?' he sa, glancing around with amusement.

'Oui, oui,' molesworth deux et moi.

'Eet eez so pretty.'

'Exquisitely so,' sa molesworth deux.

'My parents have a chateau, a flat in paris, a villa in the s. of fr. and a rolls-royce. Zizz is all you posess?'

'We have also a pen, a piece of india ruber, un morceau de papier, a cranky old car and a bag of bulls-eyes, my little cabage,' we repli. And with this riposte we zoom away into the bushes.

Things do not look good for the future chiz and mater is very cross with us ect. for our cruel and unfeeling behaviour but when she see wot armand eat she change her tune. Armand, in fakt, eat more than molesworth 2 and that is saing a v. grate deal: also we do not seme to like cotage pie, bread and butter pudding, spotted dick, corned beef and other kinds of homely food. He always zoom up to vilage shop on his bike and come back with pokets stuffed with food chiz which he eat all himself it nearly drive molesworth 2 mad.

'Last nite,' armand sa, 'i am having a beautiful dream.'

Wot can it be about? Hav he routed the beaks,

stolen GRIMES the headmaster's kane, pinched ye old matrone's gin, placed a sukkessful booby trap on the door of the master's common room. No, it is none of these things which would delite the heart of the healthy english boy. Armand hav dreamed of fresh pineaple, lobsters, duck, sweet, cheese, fruit, cream, three wines and a brandy. Well, i mean to say, wot a thing to dreme about! Anyway, give me a good suck at a tin of condensed milk every time.

Anyway, he like GURLS aussi, so something must be wrong. Anyone who can get on his bike and ride 10 miles to meet angela winterbottom becos he kno she must pass along the lane on her pony must be bats. i supose i could manage lobsters but not angela winterbottom who giggle all the time and is uterly wet. It seme, konklude the grate sage molesworth, that fr. and english are divided by more than the chanel.

GUIDE TO GROWN-UPS

Beware of addults, whether parents or beaks. They hav only one wish i.e. to make noble upright boys like them chiz. And look at them! Wot a lot, eh?

And here are the prizes for all the boys who hav not got prizes . . .

At least st. custard's turns out a finished product.

Mensam! . . . Yes, you've *got* it, Blatworthy!

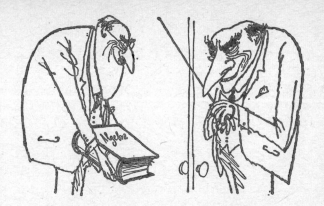

I want you to regard this as a chalenge, molesworth.

The Assyrian came down like a wolf on the fold, mogley-howard one.

Look, boys, here's Cecily come to tea.

I've no objection to him having a good hiding now and then.

MOLESWORTH TAKES OVER

Gosh chiz here's a fine state of afairs, eh? I mean, look at the world it is worse than big skool after one of our super rags full of broken desks (finest chippendale hem-hem i don't think), cries of 'you didn't,' did, didn't ect, the fluff from a million pillows and all the beetles taking refuge in the master's desk which is a poor place to choose, seeing it is full of empty beer bottles and catterpults they hav confiskated from the gallant boy fighters.

Wot would everyone say if we skoolboys behaved like the nations of the globe? I will tell you. They would sa we were stupid, crass, ignorant, hopeless, wet, weedy and sans un clue. And yet it still go on. It is time i took over. I can see it all.

Scene: A tent in Gaul, guarded with fossis and rampartibus maximus fortissimus. Labienus, Cotta, Balbus, Hanibul, Caesar, Hasdrubel and various other weeds are listening to the sweet voices of the gurls.

HANIBUL: (*at length*) gosh, wot a din it is somethink awful. How is the generalissimo toda?

CAESAR: In a filthy bate. He hav been ever since he turned good and gave up smoking. He is not the molesworth who put 99 consekutive subjects in the acc.

(*A flourish of trumpets. Enter Generalissimo molesworth*

with an old coal bucket on his tawny locks. His breath is coming in short ha-ha hee-hee you hav guessed it and he is dressed in the same.)

ALL (*acclaming*) Ave, dux!

GENERALISSIMO MOLESWORTH: And the best of luck. Wot is the situation? Does anybody kno? Put me in the piktchah. G.1?

G. 1: i was hoping *you* would put *me* in the piktchah, sirra.

G. 2 to G.99: (*in sukcession*) same here, old top.

GENERALISSIMO MOLESWORTH: oh. Carry on, then.

BRITANNICUS, A DIRTY OLD SLAVE: If i may be permitted a word, sir, the situation is quite intolerable. Porridge Court hav cocked snooks at us, spoken foully of GRIMES, our revered headmaster, called us cowardly custardians and threaten our very existence by pinching our plaing fields. They hav also attacked the ditches with javelins and spears. It really is a tremendously bad show.

GENERALISSIMO MOLESWORTH: File a complante with uno as ushaual. Who's for conkers?

(*The sweet voices of the gurls brake out agane. The generalissimo starteth.*)

Gosh, blime, i can't stand this. We march aganst porridge court! Sound the trumpets, wake the horses, prang the airports, charge ta-ran-ta-rah.

That is the beginning. Despite cries and lamentations from fotherington-tomas st. custard's declare war on porridge coury crying Pax. We must ensure there is Pax at all costs.

Scene: The same tent. Three months later.

GENERALISSIMO MOLESWORTH: Aren't we ready to move yet? Wot is the piktchah, G.1?

G.1: They are showing marylyn monro oh-ho over the naafi, sirra. Deffinitely worth a trip.

GENERALISSIMO MOLESWORTH: But didn't we declare bellum? Declare it agane.

ALL: Bellum, bellum, bellum, belli, bello, bello.

GENERALISSIMO MOLESWORTH: o.k. get cracking. Go in heah, heah and heah. Let me kno sometime how the battle goes.

G.1: O.k. sirra we will bring up the engines.

GENERALISSIMO MOLESWORTH: You don't need engines. You want catterpults. Engines pull tranes: they are 4–6–2 and 4–4–0 ect. Oh, i see. You are referring to ballista, like ensa, the siege engine? Why didn't you sa so?

(Silence except for the sweet voices of the gurls.)

And so the mitey forces of st. custard's move relentlessly in and occupy a small corner of the plaing fields. The lamentations of fotherington-tomas, who is a gurlie become louder and louder: then uno, the county council and the ratepayers association call for a cease fire. We obay.

Scene: A t.v. screen with the face of Generalissimo molesworth, blubbing.

G. MOLESWORTH: My frends, it is only in a case of national emergency that i would dare to interrupt robin hood. I come to explane the position we are in. It is grim. The skool playing field is vital to our existence. The plaing field must be free for us to come and go, freely. Where else could we be beaten 12 to nil by the village oiks, eh? Now we hav attained our objectives. The plaing fields hav been blown up by porridge court saing yar-boo and sucks. This will mean hardship. Skool sossages will be rationed, skool cheese cut by fifty per cent and lessons will continue all day. There will be less buble gum and if there ever had been any sugar that would hav been abolished too. However, it will be a matter for satisfacktion that the full supply of prunes will be maintaned. good evening.

And wot hapen then? uno, the county council and the ratepayers association anounce that they are making a police force. They sa they are giving themselves TEETH. This is a funny thing for any one to give himself but there it is. And of wot is the police force composed? It is made up as follows:

> 1 regiment of mice.
> fotherington-tomas.
> 3 tree rats (with pea shooters).

christopher robin.
The 5th brigade of rabbits.
andy-pandy.
the skool dog.

Well there you are. There hav to be a first time
and this is the best they can do and, as for us wizard
chaps, it prove something i.e. when we grow up we
will be able to make even a bigger mess than this.
So are we downharted? NO. We would not want to
be anyone else. So boo to everybody and play up
US!

THRO' HORRIDGES WITH GRAN

'I have been dealing here for 30 years,' sa gran to the
assistant at horridges stores. 'Send for mr beckwith
at once.'

Tremble, tremble quake quake how can she speke
to an Assistant in the sossage dept. like that? i mean
he is a perfect gent and wear striped trousis ect unlike
headmaster GRIMES and other beaks we could
mention and i would never dreme of ragging him.
Wot will he do? To my surprise he bow low until his
nose almost go wam on the sossage counter.

'Certainly, madam,' he sa.

End of part 1 now for the commercials, also query
wot will happen when mr beckwith arive, eh? i am
not a funk (cries of o, no, molesworth i do not think,
may you be struck ded ect.) i am the goriller of 3 B

yet i confess that i xperience a feeling of wishing to slink away and examine a nearby bakon machine. i have a feeling that mr beckwith if he arive at all will take out a gat and shoot gran to the ground. i begin to move when there is a stern cry i.e. nigel, stay where you are! There is no escape we will hav to shoot it out.

Perchance, molesworth, i sa to myself, mr beckwith will decide not to se gran? Perchance he will not obay this imperious summons?

Not a hope. mr. beckwith arive who is a kindly old man with silver hair. He is just the sort of customer to whip out a Colt and go BANG! BANG! Got you! before the sherif of dodge city can inform him that killing is WRONG. But, surprise, he also bow low to gran who fix him with an eye of steel.

'mr beckwith,' sa gran, 'i have been dealing with horridges for 30 yrs. You are aware of that?'

'Yes, yes.'

'I have here my dere grandson, nigel, the pride and aple of my eye. He is a child of grate gifts, sensitive and intcligent, a fine young gentleman.

'Observe his noble brow, his blue eyes, the aristokratick maner in which he stands.'

i mene, i sa, this is a bit much. Enuff is as good as a feast the way gran go on I mite be fotherington tomas. It is about time that mr beckwith tell the truth and state that i hav a face like a squished tomato. But he bow even lower.

'Yes, yes,' he sa, agane.

gran draw herself up to her full height.

'MR BECKWITH, WHY ARE THERE NO SOPWITHS SOSSAGES FOR MY DERE GRANDSON?'

Mr beckwith turn pale and drop upon his knees for horridges are guilty of this hideous crime. He beg for mercy and sa that he will send out specially and deliver within the hour. He even pat me on the head chiz and sa i am a dere little chap. Gran look as if she will spurn him with her foot but sweep out of the sossage dept. instead.

'Come, nigel,' she sa.

Dashed embarassing, wot? i only relate this incident becos lots of grans behave like this in shops also they talk loudly in the bus they seme to hav no idea of the finer feelings of brave noble skoolboys. Also most grans are strikt. You may be a blue-eyed child in the sossage dept. of horridges but once grans get you home it is a v. diffrent story i.e.

WHEN I WAS A GURL little boys always stood UP when a lady come into the room. WHEN I WAS A GURL little boys always leave wun for mr manners. WHEN I WAS A GURL little boys did not put their feet on the cushions ect.

And so it go on. It seme a little impertinent posh prose to ask how long ago it was when gran was a gurl, i.e. about 1066 but i refrane. I am, in fakt, pritty GOOD when gran is around as i have found that crime do not pay chiz. On the other hand you get super meals and, if you are lucky you can read an old copy of chatterbox about wee tim who is a wet and a weed. On the whole, however, it is pritty much like prison or skool which parents should remember when they decide to go to the s. of france and leave their offspring with gran.

'We are too much of a handful for the older genneration,' I muse, absent-mindedly drawing beetles on the drawing room wall. 'We are—'

'NIGEL WOT ARE YOU DOING? GO TO BED AT ONCE WITHOUT ANY SUPPER.'

Well, you see wot i mean, eh?

3

N. MOLESWORTH, ACE REPORTER

AGGRICULTURE

CLANG-PIP, CLANG-PIP once agane it is the skool bell which sumon the fatheful of st custards also the louts oiks bullies cads wets and weeds who infest the place.

'oh well,' i sa litely just like bob cherry, harry wharton etc, 'old GRIMES, the head, hav caught molesworth 2 eating his mortar board and is going to give him the swish.'

'Cheese it, molesworth,' sa peason, 'that greyfriars stuff is out of date.'

i jab a compass into gillibrand. 'OW Yaroosh Garoo,' he splutter so it is not so out of date after all.

Wot hav this to do with traktors and aggriculture? Effort, old spud! Allow me to explane. When headmaster GRIMES come into big skool he have a most unnatural smile upon his face which make it more dredful than before. Wot can be the meaning of this sinister event? Are we all to be kaned? i simply canot bear the thort, my dere, it is too much on a monday morning. i switch off and think of robin hood on t.v. . . . . *Sir guy of GRIMES is about to lash molesworth 2 whom he hav cobbed eating the king's deer when sudenly an arow WING out of the wood and split the kane in two. A figure in lincoln green emerge from Sherwood forest and vault litely over the skool roller. 'Ha, Sir guy,' sa robin moles . . .*

The dreme fade. Not for the ushual reason, i.e. a stuning blow on the head. i am aware that the rest of the skool is cheering, desks are banged, fingers are flicked and fotherington-tomas hav fanted. One would judge them to be pleased. Wot can it be? A half-hol? i switch on agane.

'And the skool we shal visit,' sa Grimes, 'is a TRAKTOR SKOOL.'

WIZZ-Oh! That is better than julius ceasar the silly old geezer ect. In fakt it is super and smashing. Wot can the day hold for us little chaps?

First we go to a traktor factory where all the men are puting the traktors together. SMASH, BIFF, BANG, WALLOP, AR-Um the noise is collosal just like st. custards on a wet saturday. Conveyor belts are zooming in all directions and there is an assembly line where chaps are bunging on wheels, engins, paint ect also whistling 'davy crocket' and working out football pools. A modern english faktory. It engage my interest and i step up to our guide with my reporter's notebook and fix him with a steely eye.

'How many parts are there in a traktor?' i rap.

'4672,*' he repli.

'Gosh!'

'And there are $11\frac{1}{2}$ miles of conveyor belts, we produce 230 traktors a day (approx) and a traktor

*******All the fakts are corect for a change.*

He hav climbed on the conveyor belt and an absent-mi

rkman is bolting him on instead of a mudguard.

come off the assembly line every 2 minits.'

'my dere, you simply stagger me.'

'Britain is the most heavily mechanised country in the world. It hav more traktors per acre than america or rusia.'

'Cheers cheers cheers hurrah for st. george and boo to everybody else . . .'

At this moment there is a suden cry. Where is molesworth 2? A hue and cry ensue. Where can he be? At last the truth is discovered he hav climbed on the conveyor belt and an absent-minded workman is bolting him on instead of a mudguard. molesworth 2 is rescued chiz more fritened than hurt (official communique) a lucky escape for a farmer who mite have got a traktor with 4673 parts one of which was molesworth 2 it would hav been a cranky old grid.

Now to the TRAKTOR skool. Wot do we see? Wizard combine harvesters, traktors, sub-soilers, ploughs and fork-lifters. Everything for the young farmer in fakt. Agane my notebook come out.

'Why do you have a skool for traktors?' i grit.

'A splendid wizard q.!' exclame the guide He turn to GRIMES. 'Wot a brany, inteligent, outstanding pupil.'

'er . . . Yes,' sa GRIMES. (*thinks:* i hav always said molesworth would turn out well. A late-developer.)

'We hav a skool for traktors,' sa the guide, 'becos it is no use for a farmer having a traktor unless he kno how to use it and how to keep it in good repare. So we trane people from all over the world how to plow, ridge, avoid soil erosion and other worthy things. The result is more of everything – wheat, beet, turnips, cabage—'

CABAGE! At the mention of the word the whole skool think of cabage and give a groan. More skool CABAGE! And full of beetles and slugs even molesworth 2 will not eat slugs.

'CABAGE?' sa molesworth 1, the ace reporter. 'i supose we shall get more spinach as well?'

'Yes, yes.'

At the very thort the skool groan agane. Wot is the use of traktors if they get more CABAGE and spinach, eh? We shall get more skool sossages next. Our guide see that he hav made a bish. 'Who would like to drive a traktor now? Our traktor can be driven by a child of eight.'

A mighty cheer rend the air.

'Goody goody,' sa fotherington-tomas, jumping up and down. 'Hullo clouds, hullo sky here i come, trusty and true, a joly farmer who plow the good rich earth, who, simple soul that he be . . .'

WAM! 91 boyish hands are raised aganst him, but it is too late.

'You look a sturdy little chap,' sa the guide to fotherington-tomas. 'You shall drive the traktor and now i want a volunteer from the masters to ride behind.' There is silence. 'How about you sir?' sa the guide to GRIMES.

'Me? Wot me?'

'Anybody else?'

With a cry like a hyena sigismund the mad maths

master spring upon the traktor and stand behind the saddle with straws in his sparse hare. fotherington-tomas grasp the steering wheel zoom the throttle and away they go cheers cheers cheers cheers. ARUM ARA ARUM mud fly in all directions and fotherington-tomas dash into a shed. Will he make it? Out the other end, turn left, zoom through a hay stack then round in a circle.

'Stop him stop him,' yell the guide.

fotherington-tomas turn three more circles and make for the open country, then reverse back scattering all, heading for the mane road. Wot will his fate be? But he hit another haystack and stop chiz chiz chiz just when it was getting interesting.

'Most stimulating,' sa sigismund the mad maths master.

'Goody goody,' sa fotherington-tomas. 'May I drive a combine now?'

Well you kno a combine it is a mighty thing which harvest the corn and put it into sacks you can imagine wot would hapen we should all be harvested and put into sacks too. Anyway, the guide sa something but it is not 'yes' it sound quite different. Conduct mark? 'Lack of control?' He seme quite pleased that we canot stay any longer.

'Any free traktors?' sa headmaster GRIMES. 'i am very poor the skool do not pay and business in jellied eels is friteful and wot with the cost of living going up—'

Agane the answer is 'no'. A pity. All the same the traktor skool was wizard and a boy of 8 *can* drive one if he is not utterly wet like fotherington-tomas. And don't forget that traktors hav helped to double the harvest of wheat in this country. Which is wizard if you like wheat. And i expect it is the same for CABAGES too. *If* you like CABAGES.

CURRENT LIVING. That is wot it is called. It is better than lat. fr. algy. geom. ect., tho, and our next visit is to an AGGRICULTURAL SHOW.

Cheers cheers zoom out of the bus and dash into a large place with a lot of cattle, sheep, implements, BEER, ice creams, fleas, straw, beetles, bottles of pepsi-cola, fat ladies and FREE LEAFLETS. In fakt it is a shambles wot with all the cows mooing and the farmers jumping about becos somerset hav won victory in the killed meat competition.

st custards descend upon the free leaflets it is every boy for himself. But molesworth 1 hav a sterner task i.e. to report the show without fear or favour. Wot do he see, eh? Look for a joly farmer going to raspberry fair ect. but only a lot of posh chaps smoking cigars. Then sudenly—

GRRHHMOOOOOOOOOOOOOOO

Gosh chiz! Jump six feet in the air and turn around to see an extraordinary sight. The objekt have a huge face, whiskers and long hare in fakt i mite be looking in a mirror and it is ME! We look at each other. Then i see a notice 'ABERDEEN ANGUS FIRST PRIZE COW also mrs joyful price for rafia work.' Promptly i grab my notebook and lick my h.b. pencil for the interview—

SOCIETY KOLUMN

ME: Yore hare look as if it hav had a shampoo and all the beetles washed out of it. Is that so?

COW: How nice of you but it look dreadful i can do nothing with it. i really must go to a new man.

ME: Yore cote is beautiful and glossy.

COW: It's simply in rags i would give my eyes for some of these farmers' wives minks they are wearing. If only my bull were not so mean.

ME: Any coment on somerset victory in home-killed meat?

COW: Poor Buttercup! Such a sad end. I knew her

Ho for sheep, traktors and
meckanical milkers.

well and such a good family. Now if you'll excuse
me i simply must have my afternoon rest . . .

Of corse cows can't talk but it just show you
should not believe everything you read in the papers.
Heigh ho and back to the show where wizard
shambles exists as fotherington-tomas hav been
prodded by mechanical fork. Ho for sheep, traktors,
meckanical milkers and the aggriculture of our land.
If it had anything to worry about it hav much more
now cheers cheers cheers, and rilly-me dilly-me.

THE FLYING MOLESMAN

'DAYVEE CROCKETT,
DAYVEE CROCKETT'
KING OF THE WILD FRONTIER.'

Thus music pour from boyish throtes, golden locks
stream in the air, and eager blue eyes are lifted to
the skies.

'BE QUIET,' yell GRIMES, the headmaster.
But no one hear him over the hideous din of this
famous song which all boys love to sing. It is only
when all boys are exorsted that GRIMES can
make himself heard.

'Boys,' he sa, smiling cruelly, 'we are going to
King's Cross station for a trip on ye olde trane, the
"flying scotsman." You are to report on the journey.'

A hideous cheer rend the air. We may hav hoped
to go on a space rocket but the 'flying scotsman' is

better than weedy lessons, especially if you hav not done yore prep. And so to King's cross . . .

All are excited and fotherington-tomas skip up and down. 'Hullo steam! hullo smoke, hullo ralway station buffet!' he sa as the porter carry our bags. Then he lean towards me and whisper, 'did you kno that queen boadicea is suposed to be buried here, eh?' Quick as a flash i see a scoop! . . .

BOADICEA DONE. BURIED at king's cross. Soon wires will be humming all over the world and ace newshawk molesworth will hav done it agane . . . but as this hav o to do with the 'Flying scotsman' i will desist. Nay, i must becos a loud-speaker in the roof boom:

'THE TRAYNE NOW STANDING AT NUMBER TWO PLATFORM IS THE 10 A.M. FOR EDIN-BURGH. GET CRACKING OR IT WILL GO WITH-OUT YOU. I WILL NOW SING A VERY FAVOURITE TUNE'

'DAYVEE CROCKETT,
DAYVEE CROCKETT
KING OF THE WILD FRONTIER ECT.'

As the wild song continue and 100 voices take it up, the st. custard's cads go forward to the engine. For we are to ride on the footplate with the driver cheers cheers cheers. 'O goody! O cheers the engine is a streamlined Pacific Number O7666655438,' sa fotherington-tomas. 'Hullo coal, hullo spade, hullo tender.' Well, there will be plenty of chances to 'do' him on this trip that is one comfort. But now for some fakts. I butonhole joe binks the driver, alias 'mad jack.'

ME: Where does the 'Flying Scotsman' stop, eh?
BINKS: i think it's newcastle but i couldn't be sure.
   Where do we stop bill, did you read the notices?
ME: Never mind. How long has it been running?
BINKS: I simply haven't a clue.
ME: Did you always want to be an engine driver?
BINKS: Grate heavens no my dere. My parents
   forced me into it when i faled c.e.

Hem-hem this is wot is called 'colour' for no news stories are true. Aktually the 'Flying Scotsman' hav been running for eighty years: it stop once at new-castle and get to edinburgh in $7\frac{1}{2}$ hrs. which is not bad as it is 393 m.*
   PEEP!
   Gracious, gracious they are whistling us up, sa joe binks, and it is ten o'clock. Do be an angel and take the brake off!
   WOMP! WOMP! WOMP! WOMP!
   i do not kno if you hav ever been on the footplate of an express but when it start it is like a big gun going off. It is louder than big school on a wet saturday and even louder than when molesworth 2 pla fairy bells on the skool piano smoke is every-where and all boys blub for mummy. The 'flying scotsman' is on its way and noone can hear them-selves speak.

* *All fakts corect for a change.*

How to get my story? Luckily i remember the essay we are always set at the end of the summer hols e.g. a day at a railway station. It go as folows viz. *'Stations are niss nice. Tranes come to stasson stashion stasion and the pasengers get out, alternatively some of the pasengers get in. The sun is shining shinning shining. There is a statshion stashon stasson mast – there is a porter on the plaff—'*

But wot is this? We are now at speed and approaching potters bar. and our coon skins are flying in the wind. On the slope beyond stevenage there was a world speed record for engines of 112 m.p.h. We are on our way north.

3.4. *First stop newcastle.—*

Chiz chiz the st. custard newshawks look as if it is the end of the first half v porridge court as they stager to the platform plafform plaform they hav had their chips. And wot is the first thing that comes to their deafened ears, eh? From the loudspeaker come

> *'DAYVEE CROCKETT,*
> *DAYVEE CROCKETT*
> *KING OF THE WILD FRONTIER ECT.'*

Now we leave joe binks and take our seats in a compartment and study a few more fakts e.g. the engine belong to the loco dept. and the rest belong to the traffick dept.

'No?' sa peason with brethless interest. 'that is the kind of thing which grip the reader. You are a born journalist, molesworth 1.'

'Do you reelly think so?'

'yes yes thou art also a measley worm and a wet but

so are many born journalists. So they are reelly from 2 depts fasscinating but so wot so wot?'

'Supose,' i sa slowly, 'they forget to fix the engine to the trane? Supose the engine arive in edinburgh and the pasengers are still sitting in king's cross? Wot then, eh?'

This conversation is interupted by the dining car attendant who ask us to take our seats for tea. Zoom

'No no go on go on.'

zoom there is a mad rush headed by molesworth 2 and we sit down to wizard toste, cakes buns ect. But i do not forget my assinement so i talk to the dining car attendant.

'No one seme to wonder how we manage in restaurant cars,' he sa, sadly. 'No one care how the food get here.'

fotherington-tomas burst out blubbing. 'i do i do' he sa.

'They don't mind that we hav to draw our food from the control dept in the cellars at king's cross. They are indifferent that we hav to turn up an hour

and a half before the trane starts. They do not care
all the cooking is done by electrissity in the kitchen.'

You could hardly expect it to be done in the
guard's van ha-ha, i sa litely. The attendant look at
me thortfully.

Who thinks of the cook when he go to the larder at
king's cross? he asks. Now we are all blubbing and
only molesworth 2 repli: i do, he sa, i am sorry i did
not go with him.

Well you kno how many prunes, radiomalts, skool
sossages he pinch all the time so i can see he is planing
a new job when we get back. He is a weed.

Now the mity trane rumble over the royal border
bridge and soon we are in scotland. we go back to our
smoker and lite up our cigs.

Hav you ever considered, peason, i sa, that we hav
been traveling north through country steeped in
hist? That the trane folow the grate north road
constructed by the romans and julius ceasar the
silly old geyser?

'good heavens, you sla me, molesworth.'

... That at darlington station stands locomotion ı
the first to run on a public railway?

'No no go on go on.'

... That they sa queen boadicea is buried at king's
cross station? But his eyes are closed and peason hav
fallen asleep chiz chiz and so hav all the rest. All the
same i let my mind pla upon dremes and fancies
(posh prose) of the past.

caesar, livy, romulus and remus are sitting in a compartment.

CAESAR: We were ten minutes late at Eboricum and they call this a railway.

LIVY: Travelling on business i supose?

CAESAR: i am going up to attack the picts and scots. i hav finished with the gauls and hav attacked so many ramparts and ditches in Italy it will be a nice change.

ROMULUS: Scotios sunt weeds.

CAESAR: Be quiet, boy, and do not put yore nom in the acusative it's not grammer. Also stop sucking that pabulum. Did you kno that queen boadicea is buried at King's Cross station?

LIVY: No? How fasscinating!

(*He falls aslepe as j. caesar continue and do not wake until Romulus and Remus comence to sing an old roman ditty* e.g.

> '*DAYVEE CROCKETUS*
> *DAYVEE CROCKETUS*
> *REX OF THE WILD FRONTIER.*'

The dreme fade.

But wot is this? We are nearing our journey's end and steaming into edinburgh station. It is five heures et demie and the 'flying scotsman' is on time cheers cheers cheers. We hav traveled 393 miles in $7\frac{1}{2}$ heures. And wot is the first thing we hear as we get down on the platform plafform plaform? It is e.g.

> '*DAYVEE McCROCKET*
> *DAYVEE McCROCKET*
> *KING OF THE WILD FRONTIER.*'

And tomorrow we return to king's cross where, of corse, they sa queen boadicea is buried.

TAKING WINGS

It is a quiet day in the news room at st. custard's. 2 tipewriters are chatering, 16 boys are chatering harder, peason is dreamily soaking ink from the well onto his blotch, gillibrand carve his initials on his desk, fotherington-tomas (our litterrary critick) read t.s. eliot and the fearful News Editor GRIMES lounge at his desk chiz chiz chiz. Sudenly a well-known figure enter, his hat is on the back of his head and a cig droop from his lips. He slouch over and sit on GRIMES desk. It is ace-reporter nigel moles-worth cheers cheers cheers he fear nobody.

'MOLESWORTH!' yell GRIMES.

'Y . . . Y . . . Y . . . Yep, Sir.'

'Don't sa "Yep".'

'N . . . N . . . N . . . Nope, sir.'

'Or "Nope".'

'Y . . . Y . . . Yep, sir.'

This can go on for ever and GRIMES kno that he canot browbeat dauntless, questing newshawk ect. He canot . . . WAM! the ruler come down on molesworth's fingers chiz chiz chiz moan moan.

'MOLESWORTH i hav a story for you. Get something on london airport. How it work, wot it do ect.'

'Wot, sir, me, sir. Oh no, sir, i mean to sa, sir, that's a chiz, sir.'

'Get going boy! Wot are you waiting for? Do you

want a condukt mark? You are slack, idle, insubordinate, weedy wet and a weed ect ect.'

ZOOOOOOOOOOM!

Two hours after leaving london the car which cary the st. custard's reporting team crawl past london airport, turn left, through the tunel and with a screech of brakes pull up at the door. 'Hullo planes, hullo passengers, hullo sky!' sa a gurly voice so you can guess that fotherington-tomas is here also peason, grabber, gillibrand and molesworth 2 it is no wonder the porters think we are bound for belgrade and the guide who meet us make as if to run awa.

'Wot go on here?' i rap, licking my old h.b. 'Tell us the whole story and make it snappy.'

'You are "pasenger-processed".'

This sound v. much like wot go on behind the bushes at st. custard's when a new bug hav been cheeky you kno we give him the works. But at the airport they just pass you through a chanel as they call it and, by the end, this is very much the same thing.

'Imagine you are pasengers,' sa the guide. 'First you go up to this here desk (grammer) and hav tickets checked ect. Then yore baggage is put on a conveyor belt for the Customs, while you go up to the Concourse on a moving staircase to yore apropriate chanel. The grate thing about the system is that nothing can go wrong.'

O-ho O-ho i think you are uterly wet if you think

nothing can go wrong with st. custard's about you wate. As usual i am rite all the reporters zoom up the moving staircase then charge ta-ran-ta-rah down the other it is beter than the pleasure gardens and it is FREE. It take the loudspeaker system to get them back.

'WILL ALL BOYS ATACHED TO ST. CUSTARD'S *KINDLY* COLECT THEIR MARBLES AND PEASHOOTERS. TAKE LEAVE OF THEIR FRINDS AND PROCEED TO CHANNEL 6?'

'Shan't,' sa molesworth 2.

'WOT'S THAT?' sa the loudspeaker, 'WILL ST. CUSTARD'S BOYS PROCEED TO CHANNEL 6 *IMMEDIATELY*.'

'Yar boo sucks.'

'LOOK 'ERE I DON'T WANT ANY MORE OF YORE LIP GET CRACKING OR ELSE.'

This, my dears, is language we can understand and it hav the desired effect. We asemble at the door where a beautiful AIRGURL is standing she is absolutely fizzing more lovely even than prudence entwistle the under matron. My eyes pop and mouth open but all i can say is 'g . . . g . . . gug.'

'London airport,' sa the guide, 'process over 2 million passengers every year, in fakt, to be acurate ast year it was 2,683,605.'*

---

* *All the fakts are CORECT. They have been certified by the board of rade, ticked by Sigismund the Mad Maths Master and approved by the lassblowers union cheers.*

'g . . . g . . . gug.'

'It can handle 30 planes an hour at peak period and over 119,000 each year. It is the busiest airport in the world in space. It hav 6 runways, the longest being number one which is 9,300 feet long.'

'g . . . g . . . gug.'

'Are you listening, boy?'

I come to with a start and take my eyes of the beautiful AIRGURL. She hav a smile on her face can it be for me? Now gosh she is bending towards me can it be true? But wot do she sa? Her words are torture, e.g. 'You seme unhapy, little fellow. Do not cry for mummy she would not like that. Let me take you by the handy-pandy.'

And she do chiz chiz chiz chiz while all st. custards cheer. Well anybody who take *me* by the handy-pandy are taking a risk, they are never savoury hem-hem but i supose AIRGURLS hav to be tuough. And so, hand in hand, the little toddler by her side, she lead the way into the CUSTOMS. i shall never live this down.

CUSTOMS! brrh brrh it is like the cave in ali baba when the thieves come back quake quake wot will they do to you? and WOT is this? molesworth 2 hav come through on the moving belt with the bagage and they hav laid him on the counter. Well, if they make him declare wot is inside him i.e. 69 lickorice allsorts, 3 bubble gum, bits of bungy and 9 skool sossages they will get wot is coming to them. But i have not time to concentrate becos i am standing in front of a man who look like capt. hook

'Come on, cough it up. We can tell when you are lying.'

in weedy peter pan and rap the counter with his hook.

'Hav you read this? Anything to declare? Come on, cough it up. We can tell when you are lying. No compasses, watches, bungy, blotch, cigs, bikes, magic lanterns, brownie No o or other dutiable goods? No cribs, woollen pants, white mice, caterpillers or doodle bugs?'

He glare at me and I meet his eye quake quake i am about to confess when AIRGURL sa: 'This little boy is v. sad for his mummy.' Thwarted he scribble rude things hem-hem in red chalk. 'Take him to Immigration.' SAVED! but at wot cost! Immigration is O.K. they just check yore crimes

and look at yore passport and then you are through
and free to wing away into the blue ect.

Here i check my men. Of eight gallant souls only 2
hav got through. e.g. me and fotherington-tomas.
Weep hem-hem for the rest who have perished on
the miserable journey which is the worst in the world.

Hist! but now wot is this? Still grasping my handy-
pandy the AIRGURL take me and fotherington-
tomas to a door. She open it and take us through and
wot grisly sight meet my tired eyes? It is a
NURSERY chiz chiz chiz chiz full of rocking
horses and ickel pritty babies. On all sides are teddy
bears and sea-saws 'O goody goody,' sa fotherington-
tomas skipping weedily. 'Let us pla with the bears!' I
turn to escape but the door hav closed. TRAPPED!
Trapped with fotherington-tomas, a Nurse, 16
babies, 90 coloured balls, 56 teddy bears and a pedal
car it is an uggly predicament.

There is only one course i shall hav to fite my way
out. 'Listen,' i drawl, drawing a gat, 'the first baby
that draw a bead on me gets plugged, see? I'm kinda
hostile to babies and my finger mite slip on the
trigger.'

WAM! A mighty coloured ball which weigh 2
tons strike me on the nose and the party get ruough
balls and teddy bears fly in all directions, a baby fly
off the see-saw and strike his pritty locks on the
ceiling and the NURSE fante. Pausing only to
shoot out the lights i make good my escape. Outside
the guide is waiting.

'The London airport nursery service for children

in transit is quite free. There children may be left in the care of a trained nurse and there are see-saws, shiny toys, teddy bears and baby's bottle can be quickly prepared.'

'G . . . g . . . gug.' I sa.

And so with this sobering thort we leave London Airport which is joly d. reely and and may be completely finished one day and return to the gloom and beetles of our alma mater chiz.

4

.I AM GOING TO BE GOOD

HERE WE GO AGANE!

O wild west wind thou breath of autumns being thou from whose unseen presence the leaves dead are driven like gostes from an enchanter fleeing. Posh, eh? i bet you 6d. it fooled you. 'molesworth at his rolling best. Sonorus and sublime' i expect you said Aktually it is not me it is a weed called shelley and i copied it from the peotry book.

'Why?' sa molesworth 2 who zoom up like the wet he is. 'Why copy peotry when you mite be buzzing bricks, conking me on the napper or braking windows with yore air pistol go on tell me o you mite.'

'Becos,' i tell him, 'it autumn and the long hols are nearly over. Soon we shall be back at SKOOL.'

At these words he burst out blubbing and will not be comforted. I confess there hav been many times when the thort of GRIMES, the masters, the bullies cads, snekes wets and weeds would hav depressed me too. But not this time.

I AM GOING TO BE GOOD THIS TERM.

i will tell you how this hapened. The other day i am fed up with tuoughing up molesworth 2 and am stooging about saing wot shall i do mum wot shall i do eh?

To this she gives various replies i.e.

(a) *go for a walk.*

(b) *pla with your toys.*

(c) *watch t.v. childrens hour ect.*

none of these are acceptable to me so in the end she make a sugestion so rude hem-hem i canot print it here. It is thus i find myself locked in the atick until teatime chiz chiz chiz, and find gran's old book called chaterbox 1896. There is o to do so i turn its weedy pages and read the story of wee tim:

> *'wee tim is riding in his grandpater's cariage as staunch and sturdy a litle felow as ever you would wish to see. Sudenly he see an old lady who is carying a heavy basket and he clutch his grandpater's knee. 'Granpa granpa,' he sa, 'can we not let this pore old lady ride in our cariage, eh? She is so weak and frale.' Wot a good kind thort! His fierce grandpa sa 'O.K. tim even though i am an earl let us take her for a ride . . .'*

(molesworth thinks: this is where the story get craking. Now wee tim will hit her with a COSH and pinch wot is in the basket while boris the foul coachman look on with a cruel grin. But no!)

> *'Will you ride with us, old lady?' sa tim and wot a pikture he looked with his long golden curls! 'Thank you young sir,' she sa. 'But i canot ride in the carriage of an earl.' 'He is a good earl,' sa tim, 'even though he look like that.' 'And i,' she sa, 'am really a rich old lady and becos you hav been good and gentle i will leave you my fortune when i die . . .'*

Coo ur gosh i mean to sa if that is wot you get for being good it is worth it it is easier than the pools. I look back on my condukt in the hols. Hav it been all it should be?

scene: the molesworth brekfast table.
ME: gosh chiz kippers again this is worse than skool.
FATHEFUL NAN: get on, nigel, you are ungrateful.

Aktually it is not me it is a weed called Shelley.

The pore boys would be glad to have nice kippers for breakfast.
MOLESWORTH 2: Yar boo and sucks molesworth 1 have a face like a flea.
ME: Et tu, weed, thrice over and no returns.
(*A kipper fly through the air*).

FATHEFUL NAN: No little gentleman thro kippers, nigel.

MOLESWORTH I: Then i will thro korn flakes instead. Ha ha ha witty boy ha ha ha ect. . . .

i blush with shame at the memory of this unsavoury incident and *let's face it, my dears*, it was only one of many. Would wee tim have thrown a kipper at molesworth 2? Would he hav been cheeky to fatheful nan? I doubt it very much. He would hav given his kipper to the pore boys . . . O woe i am a weed chiz! Next term i will alter my ways. Already i can pikture the scene at st. custard's:

a thortful figure is walking among the dead beetles crushed biskuits and old buns which litter the skool passage. He is reading a peotry book.

MOLESWORTH I: The asyrian came down like a wolf on the fold ect. . . . Wot a luvley poem! To think that even a term ago i drew tadpoles all over it and wrote 'turn to page 103 if my name ect!' How can i hav done such a thing? The asyrian came down . . .

At this moment a huge mob of cads, snekes, oiks, tuoughs, oafs and skool dogs charge ta-ran-ta-rah like the light-brigade all covered with marmalade in my direction.

MOLESWORTH I: Silence! (*There is a hush*). Boys, this is foul condukt. You are ragging in the passage an offence under section 88888/b/107 of the skool rules. Go back to yore desks and be good in future. (*They slink awa with bowed heads.*)

GRIMES the headmaster hav been silently

observing this good DEED and he pat me on th
head make me head of the skool instead o
grabber and give me mrs joyful prize for rafi
work.

But, you kno, wot will really hapen? It will b
quite different i am afraid and will go like this.

*Scene: The klassroom. Enter master for lat. lesson
molesworth 1 hav all his books out, pensils sharp
AND BUNGY at the ready.*

ME: Good morning, dere sir. i hope you slept well

BEAK: (thinks) A trap! (He aim a vicious blow
    Take that, you dolt. Do you think you can rag me
    the scurge of the skool?

ME: i forgive you, sir You look pale you hav drunk
    BEER last night. May i get you a pil?

BEAK: Stand on yore chair, molesworth. Any more
    and you will get 6!

ME: Do not open that desk, sir, it is full of old
    cucumbers put there by i kno not whom.

BEAK: Enuff! Wate for me outside.

(*A vale is drawn over the foul proceedings.*)

Am i rite in this foul proffecy? Shall it alter my
determination to be like wee tim? Shall i shake in my
resolution? onely time will revele all – wate fellow
weeds, with baited breath, and you mite catch a
wopper, ha. ha.

Hay ho! Hullo birds! Hullo clouds! Hullo, skool dog! Hullo, sirup of figgs! Hullo, potts and pilcher fr. primer!

Who is this who skip weedily along the skool passage and out towards the den of ye olde skoole pigge? One would really hav thort it was fotherington tomas so gay is he, so lite-harted. There, dere reader, you make a big mistake as c. dickens (auther of d. Coperfield the book of the film) would sa. No, dere, gentle reader who may chance to con these pages with so much sympathy ect, you make one helluva big mistake. You are way, way out, coyottes. It is i, n. molesworth, the ex-curse of st. custards, who skip weedily, who cry hay-ho, hay-ho ect. And wot hav i being doing, eh?

FLASHBACK! 2 minits ago.

N. MOLESWORTH: Matronne, i have brought you this pressed leaf. May i do yore flowers?

MATRONNE: (*reaching for her gat*) Scram, scruff! O i will do you!

N. MOLESWORTH: i forgive you, matronne, for uncouth words. A still tongue in a wise head.

MATRONNE: Git!

N. MOLESWORTH: i will, indeed. A rolling stone gathers no moss. Likewise, procrastination is the thief of time.

MATRONNE: *YAR!*

N. MOLESWORTH: As you please. An empty barrel
makes the most noise.
(*exit with a courteous bow.*)

It is a strange, lonely world when you are
GOOD. Is it my fault that i hav been practising my
handwriting in the copy books? Now i kno wot pore,
pore basil fotherington-tomas, that wet and weed,
hav gone through. People seme to avoid me – no
friendly hale of darts and inkpots comes my way.
Even molesworth 2 refuses my buble-gum and masters pat me on the head.

*YET i MUST KEPE TO MY CHOSEN
ROAD.*

But, soft, wot is this? It is peason, my grate frend,
who worketh upon some strange contraption near the
pigge den. Wot mischief can he be up to?

'Hullo, peason,' i sa. 'The devil finds work for idle
hands. Wot is that?'

'Nothing,' he repli.

'if't be nothing, yet 'tis something, for nothing is
not but wot something semes (shakespere)' i riposte,
litely. 'Yet if't be something—' He buzz a brick at
me. No matter, i try agane.

'Go on, peason, you mite tell me go on, o you mite
the same to you and no returns.'

'you would not be interested,' he grate, turning a
nut with his spaner. 'Nowadays you are a weed, a
wet and uterly wormlike. Gone are the days when
we invented the molesworth/peason lines machine
together.'

'It hav a good streme-line effect and neat basket work. i like the way the electronick brane give easy control and at the same time there is wide vision and plenty of lugage space. Good points are—'

It is a strange, lonely world
when you are GOOD.

He buzz another brick and, sorowfully, i depart. Ah me, where is there to go? Who else luv me but my old frende the skool pigge, who hav never let me down? Hurrah, hurrah, he leap to greet me and place his piggy paws on the sty wall. He take my buble-gum graciously and lick my hand. i recite a poem i hav written e.g.

O pigge, you are so beautiful!
I luv yore snouty nose!
ect.

n.b. pigs are the cleanest animals in the world, although i sometimes think there are exceptions.

And so, refreshed and strengthened, i return once agane into the wicked world of st. custard's where peason is stil at work. Wot can it be?

Is it:

An atommic fast-bowling machine?

An automatick golekeeper?

A loudspeker for calling 'Fire!' in the middle of maths lessons?

A measles-rash injector?

Curiosity overcome me and i return.

'No honestly, peason, word of honour cross my hart fingers uncrossed and pax tell me, rat, wot it is or i will uterly tuough you up.'

'That is better, clot. Now i will tell you – it is a MASTER TRAP.'

Hurrah! Hurrah! A trap for beaks. Wot a wizard wheeze! Gosh, absolutely super and smashing! Good show! Charge ta-ran-ta-rah! Dozens of master – lat masters fr. geom. algy. div masters all caught and eliminated. And it work for mistresses, too! But chiz wot am i saing? For a moment i thort the world mite be safe in future for children – i must be careful.

'Kindly explane,' i sa, a triffel stiffly (but no enuff to make him withdraw into the silence usuhually so alien to him).

He tell me all. There is a bait of lat. books attracted iresistibly the beak creep stealthily in through the door and before he can get to ex.1. th trap hav closed. A see-saw tip him into a cold bat and an endless belt take him to a third chambe where he get six from the automatick caning machine.

'Yes, yes,' i sa, excitedly. 'Wot then! Wot devilish fate waits for them then?'

'They die sloly on a diet of skool food!'

'Gosh, yes! Or you mite hang a skool sossage eternally out of reach.'

'That would be no punishment, oaf. And you are lucky. i am going to make my first experiment with *YOU*!'

Too late i see the plot, chiz! A dozen hands with beetles and earwigs drawn on them scrag me. The leader is grabber, the tete de la skool. 'Make haste slowly,' i yell. 'Too many cooks spoil the broth; Help; Rescue.' But whereas in the old days fifty trusty boys would hav leaped from the thickets at the sound – today none come. None at all. And robin hood had better take note of it. i am pushed towards the infernal trap and my DOOM IS SEALED.

But wot is this? My trusty frende the skool pigge hav got there first. Before they can stop him he is inside: he eat the lat. books: enjoy the bath, the caning machine tickle him litely, he wolf the skool food and with one heave of his mitey flanks he knock the whole machine for SIX! Cheers, cheers, cheers i am saved. But wot a narow shave, eh? That nite i rite carefully in my dere copy book

Virtue is its own reward

'I hear you're rustlin' raffia work, pardner.

'You're so right,' sa fotherington-tomas. 'So true, so true! Hullo, clouds! Hullo sky!'

This all needs a lot of thort.

SO FAR SO GOOD

It is evening after prep at st. custard's. The curtanes hav been drawn, the gas lites are popping merrily and the crow hav long since gone to its nest, tho where else it could go to i do not kno. In every nook and crany, knee-deep in blotch pelets, bits of bungy, old lines and pages of deten the gay little chaps enjoy there freedom. Some toste sossages over the gas mantle, others, more adventurous, swing upside down on the chandeleres. The air echo with cries of *pax, unpax, fains, roter, shutup,* and *the same to you with no returns.* WOW-EEEEEE sa molesworth 2 zooming past as a jet bomber.

But who is this quiet student who reads The book of berds and there eggs, eh? It is me, molesworth 1 believe it or not, for i hav determined to be GOOD and it is easy pappy and absolutely o to it at all. E.g. soon i put down my book, mark the place with an old pressed leaf, put it in my tidy desk and make my way quietly to the study of GRIMES the headmaster. *Knock tap tap tap!*

Wot is it, molesworth? sa GRIMES, looking up from his pools.

i hav been reading a most interesting book, sir. It is called berds and there eggs. Take the jackdaw, sir

It frequents parks, old buildings and often perform aerial acrobaticks. It hav a propensity for hiding food and other objects. Eggs ushually 4 to 6.

yes, yes, molesworth, indeed? Thank you for the information. Now—

Sometimes, however, sir, only 2 eggs are to be found. The linet, on the other hand – shall i tell you about the linet?

Some other time, molesworth. i am very busy now. times are hard how about 5 bob till tuesday?

(*Thinks: it is worth a try. A mug is born every minit.*)

Here is a pound, sir, i sa, o forget yore gratitude it would be a pore hart who did not aid an old frend in distress. It is a gift. If you want any good deed done agane just let me kno.

(*GRIMES thinks: stone the crows who would hav thort it? A hem-hem plaster saint. No need to take out the old whelk stall this week now.*)

And so it go on. that is just one example. Another thing i hav become a swot and a brane. I am top in lat, hist, algy, geom, div. ect.

Brave, proud and fearless molesworth 1 can face world safe in the knoledge that SWOTING ALWAYS PAYS.

Scene: a t.v. studio, poorly furnished, a table with three legs, lit by a candle in a botle. An interviewer in rags come forward.

INTERVIEWER: This is the 960 million quid programme. Who is the next contestant wot subjeck do you choose?

Sᴛ. M. it is i. wigan, lancs. i certainly do. i would. me and the wife will certailny hope to. History.

Iɴᴛᴇʀᴠɪᴇᴡᴇʀ: Half a mo. Wate for me to ask the q's. Who burned the cakes?

Sᴛ. M. Who pinched the cakes, you mean, molesworth 2, of corse.

Iɴᴛᴇʀᴠɪᴇᴡᴇʀ: You hav won 6000 quid would you car to go for the jakpot? Go into the box can you hear me ect. Now for 960 quid wot berd frequents parks, does aerial acrobaticks, hides food and usually lay 4 to 6 eggs, eh?

Sᴛ. M. The – um – o gosh it's ur-er choke gosh garble.

Iɴᴛᴇʀᴠɪᴇᴡᴇʀ: i'm sorry. i'm very sorry. i'm very sorry indeed. The answer was – A JACKDAW!

(*Exit st. m. blubbing on the arm of a beautiful GURL.*)

Well, there you are. Being GOOD is pappay. Try it. Try it toda. Try it brighter, try it whiter, try it with or without a hole in the family size. But wot is this? As i walk upon my pious way i come upon a MASTER who bendeth over. He is a sitting target. Wot a chance! With foot drawn back molesworth bare his fangs. Will he sukumb to temptation?

(*see another daring, palpittating instalment in our next issue.*)

THE KARACKTER KUP

'Boys,' sa GRIMES, the headmaster, smiling horibly, 'the time have come to present the scrimgeour kup for good karackter. This is never an easy kup to award' (of course not, it is ushually at the pornbrokers) 'becos there must be no doubt either in my mind or those of the staff' – he give an even more horible smile at the thugs seated around – 'that the winner is WORTHY of this supreme honor. The choice hav to be a most careful one ect.'

Aktually i do not see the dificulty. If you look at the 56 gallant little pupils of st. custards, each with his own peculiar ways, it is easy, pappy to devise a SYSTEM. You simply get rid of them in this way i.e. there are: 5 squits, 9 snekes, 19 cribbers, 2 maniaks, 3 bookmakers, 4 swots, 11 cig. smokers. Total 53.

Chiz this leaves only one pupil to whom the kup can possibly be awarded. Well, you kno, i mean to sa, i hav been joly GOOD lately and sucking up to the beaks. Obviously this fakt hav been noted. GRIMES continue:

'The boy who win this kup must be noble, upright, brave, fearless, intreppid and honnest. He must not have been afrade to stick up for wot he kno to be right. He must protekt the weak. He must luv the highest when he see it.'

Oh come on, gosh chiz this is going a bit far. i blush to the roots.

'Every boy at st custard's,' continue GRIMES, 'must search himself to see if he comes up to these high standards and if he do not the pot is not his. Hav he been a help to the masters?'

Well, that one is easy. Look wot hapened only yesterday.

Scene: Klassroom of 3B, early dawn. A pupil stands on guard with a sten gun, the rest snore at their desks. Outside a burd sings sweetly.

A beak drags himself in to his desk.

BEAK: Gosh blime, i feel terible.

MOLESWORTH: Pore sir, you have missed brekfast

The boy who win this kup must be noble, upright, brave, fearless, intreppid and honnest.

Let me get you some skool fish or a nice runny egg. (*Takt, but the beak do not seme to fancy my sugestion. He shudereth and groweth pale.*)

BEAK: Ugh. Wot lesson is it? I thort you was all due

for woodwork in the carpentry shed. You can go
along there if you like.

MOLESWORTH: Oh, no, sir. We prefer to stay with
you and do our peotry.

BEAK: i was afraid of it. Gillibrand, say yore prep.

GILLIBRAND: Who, sir, wot me, sir.

BEAK: Wot was the name of the famous peom of
which you were required to learn 24 lines?

GILLIBRAND: Search me, sir.

BEAK: (*some of his old fire reviving*) i do not wish to
search you, gillibrand, i mite be appaled at wot i
should find.

(*Ha-ha-ha-ha-ha-ha-ha-ha from all, gillibrand struggle
to his feet, his mouth open like a fish, he stare, he stammer, he
scratcheth his head and the ushual shower of beetles fall out.*)

You seme nonplussed, gillibrand. Can it be that
you were drawing H-bombs during prep?
TAKE A DETEN. Now which of you scum
can sa the peom?

MOLESWORTH: (*flipping his fingers like bulet shots,
dancing on the points of his tiny toes.*) Oh, gosh, sir
Please, sir. Gosh, sir, can i, sir?

BEAK: Ah, molesworth. i had not thort of you
heretofor as one keen on the arts. Let us see. Sa
prep.

(*molesworth stand to attention, fingers in line with th
seam of his trousis, eyes straight ahead.*)

MOLESWORTH: 'THE SAND OF DEE BY
C. KINGSLEY.'

O Mary, go and call the catle home.
And call the catle home.

And call the catle home,
Across the sands o' dee.
The western wind was wild—

BEAK: (*hastily*) That's enuff, molesworth, v.g.v.g.,
indeed.

MOLESWORTH: – and dank wi fome,
And all alone went she.
The creeping tide came up along the sand,
and o'er and o'er—

BEAK: well done molesworth joly good ten out of ten
you can stop now.

MOLESWORTH: – the sand,
And round and round the sand,
As far as eye could see:
The blinding mist came down and hid the land,
And never home came she.

(*fotherington-tomas burst out blubbing*)

O, is it weed, or fish, or floating hair?—

BEAK: Thank you, molesworth, thank you. excellent.

(*But nothing can stop me. i continue to the end of the peom
despite a hale of ink darts. At the conclusion i bow low and
strike my nose upon the desk. All look at me as if amazed.*)

Yes, i think i may sa i hav been a help to the
masters the kup is as good as mine. Wot else?
GRIMES looks around.

'Hav he been a help to the other members of the
huge staff to whom i owe so much? (i.e. about 9
million quid back wages.) Hav he helped our very
overworked skool gardener? And matron – how do he
and she get on?'

All too well, old top, if you are thinking of PRUDENCE ENTWHISTLE, the glamorous under-matron. But it must be MATRON herself, who look like a gunman's moll in a gangster pikture. But even here my record is good—

Scene: Matronne's room, the doors of ye olde physick cupboard are open.

MOLESWORTH: i have been reading of the labours of hercules, matronne, may i clean out yore cupboard? . . . Wot hav we here in the syrup of figgs bot? It smells like G-I-N . . . and wot can these BEER bottles be doing, as if hidden behind the radio-malt? . . . I will arrange them neatly in the front row . . . And wot is this which look like the skeleton of a boy chained to the wall . . . ect. O.K. there, you see. Now for the Kup.

'The winner must be of excellent repute, (o come, sire). Talented, (o fie!). Inspired.' (Enuff. You sla me.)

'And so,' sa Grimes smiling more horibly than ever, 'i hav no hesitation in awarding the kup to GRABBER.'

Well its the old story. A fat cheque and you can fix anything but right, i supose, will triumph in the end. In the meantime o mary go and call the catle home ect, or go and do something, i am fed up.

5

COO UR GOSH!

I LUV GURLS

Coo ur gosh i expect this is a bit of a shock especially for the gurls. As you kno it hav long been an open secret in 3b that i never intend to get maried. This hav been becos if you get maried it hav to be to a GURL chiz and hitherto my conviction hav been that GURLS are uterly wet and weed-struck. But this is Xmas the season of luv and goodwill cheers cheers crackers crak berds sing balloons pop and the fur from a milion davy crocket hats fly through the air.

AND SO as I sit here biting grate chunks from my old h.b. (n.b. why do not pencil makers produce a pencil out of buble gum, eh?) anyway as i sit here write these fateful words which may cut me off for ever from my felow oiks, cads, bulies, and dirty roters – i am determined to LUV GURLS.

'Oh goody,' sa fotherington-tomas who see wot my old hand hav written, 'I knew you would come round to my point of view, molesworth. Wot sort of gurls do you like?'

'All of them,' i repli. 'i shall spare myself nothing.'

'Even gurls who giggle?'

'Yes.'

'Even gurls who recite weedy rhymes i.e. *higldy piggledy i solicity umpa-la-ra-jig?*'

'Yes, yes.'

'Gurls with skipping ropes who sa "*Salt vinegar mustard peper* ect?" '

'Yes, but you are trying me hard, fotherington-tomas, very hard indeed.'

'Oh, goody. molesworth luvs gurls with skipping ropes.'

peason pass by with his face covered with ink splodges as per ushual. He faint dead awa and have to be taken up to matron.

It is only now that i see wot this mean and ponder on the nature of the feminine gender hem hem. First of all, there seme to be as many kinds o gurls as there are licorice allsorts i.e.

GURLS WHO STARE. This is a very comon type. When a brave noble and fearless boy is engaged on some super project as it mite be making a stink bomb poo gosh or a man-trap for a master the GURL come up and look at him. She sa nothing She just stand there looking soppy. The boy hop she will scram but she do not. The boy wishes to sa g and skit but maners prevent him and soon the master hand which is engaged on the task grows nervou He move off to another project. The gurl follow h canot get rid of her. Finally she speak. She sa 'One-two-three-four-five-six-sevving.' That is all. Is she bats or wot? i shal find it hard to luv these.

JOLLY HOCKEY GURLS. These gurls wear gym tunics and hav bulging muscles, they line the touchline and shout, 'Hurrah for Coll!' This is worse than at st. custard's where we sa 'go it grabber you'll never score. Wot a pass, man. buck up yore ideas.'

Hockey gurls luv their school and if hermione misses a biff at gole in the cercle she hav let the whole place down. As it is falling down anyway this do not mater very much. On satterdays after a glorious victory over st. minniver's coll for ladies (without millicent at right half, too! Water on the knee the old trubble) they all sing the skool war cry:

> *HURRA for bat!*
> *Hurra for ball!*
> *Hurra for crosse and lax*
> *And all.*
> *Forty years on we'll still be chums.*
> *Ta-ran-ta-rah for st. etheldrums.*

(all copyright reserved by miss edwina prinknash, headmistress. Send stamped addressed envelope with O for 1/3.).

TOUGH GURLS. Believe it or not all gurls are not edducated at colls ect. Some there be (posh prose hem-hem) who hav not had the advantages of a pater on the verge of suicide trying to pay the fees. Such a one (it gets posher and posher, eh?) such a one is Ermintrude you kno the one who likes boiled sweets better if they hav been dropped on the carpet. ermintrude hav not washed for several years oh wot a thing wot a thing. Also she hang up-side down on the railings and shout 'hi liberace' as you pass chiz chiz chiz. The only thing is to ignore gurls like these and when she buzz a conker at you

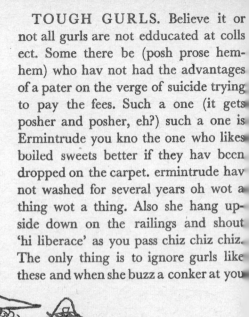

pretend the incident hav not hapened. Still, this is dificult when she also refer to molesworth 2 as 'm bruther george.'

Of corse i could go on becos there are many mor types of gurls – fat gurls, gurls with dollies, boss gurls and, on some occasions, gurls who are beter a

Such a one is Ermintrude.

essons than you. ('Oh, nigel, don't you really know
the ablative singular of armiger?' I don't supose you
even kno what it *means*.')

But this thing must not go too far. Imagine wot
would hapen at st. custard's if we were like gurls and
got a CRUSH on somebody. e.g.

FOTHERINGTON-TOMAS: oh, nigel, may i take
  yore books to the fr. class this morning?

NIGEL: foolish little thing. Peason hav already
  offered.

FOTHERINGTON-TOMAS (*blubbing*): oh.

NIGEL: never mind. You may wash the tanks and
  tractors which i hav drawn off my bungy.

FOTHERINGTON-TOMAS: Oh, goody! and may I
  clean out yore locker for you?

NIGEL: at yore own risk.

And so it go on. ANYWAY, gurls are jolly d.
They are pritty, super and smashing. Wot would we
young chaps do without them at xmas parties, eh?
Well, there'd be a lot more jelly and trifle to go
round and, whether you like it or not, you hav to
put up with them. So make the best of them.

n.b. any offers of mariage as the result of this will be considered in strikt rotation.

DANSEY DANSEY

The fell words are spoken chiz they fall upon my weedy shoulders like GRIMES lash, they strike a super shuder in my sole. Wot can these words be, eh? They are words which every brave, noble and fearless boy heard in his time i.e. when Mum sa swetely: 'It is time, nigel, you learned to dance.'

Any boy, except fotherington-tomas, hav the answer to this. 'No, mater, I won't, nothing will make me, i won't won't won't ect.' In the end, however, he always find himself in a weedy dancing klass sliding across the polished floor in shiny dancing pumps with darling bows on them chiz chiz chiz.

In fakt, come to think of it, there are not many times in his life when a weed is free from dancing klasses. It begin almost as soon as he can patter on his 2 tiny feet and his mum admire his long golden curls. There he is plaing with ratle and saing 'goo over the top of his pla pen when his mum sneke up behind him and stick a gat in his ribs: 'o.k. blue eyes we're going to dancing klass. Get moving and no funny business.' The pore baby hav no answer to this and he hav to submit while he is dressed in a velve suit chiz little todling shoes chiz chiz and look like little lord fauntleroy chiz chiz chiz. Then he i zoomed in a high-powered car to the klass.

Pikture the sordid scene with anxious mums, weedy little gurls with ribbons in their hair and 36 fauntle-roys of whom YOU are one. Enter a huge woman flexing her muscles who beam britely and sa: 'Now we're all going to be little mice and little rats . . . no, let's change our mind . . . not little rats, let's be GRATE BIG RATS . . . Tippy-toes, nigel, tippy toes . . . *You* ort to kno how to be grate big rat . . . in time to the musick . . . clap, clap, . . . now alto-gether jump into the air!'

Where else do she expect a tiny to jump, eh? Into he big drum? Though if he wear a fauntleroy suit it vould be much beter if he did. But you see wot i mean, felow suferers? You're hardly born before you hav to dansey-dansey. The next attempt is made at a ater age when yore mater try it on once agane to presuade yore stuborn boyish nature by swete reason.

Scene: The molesworth brekfast table. Pater and mater resent: molesworth 2 eating the cereal with fine relish ha-ha. molesworth 1 sit corektly a smile flitting litely akross his inely moulded features.

MATER: But if you don't learn, nigel, how will you be able to dance with GURLS at parties?

ME: i shall manage to face that kalamity with composure, mummy.

MATER: (*to pater*) Ortn't he to learn to dance, my dere.

PATER: Eh?

MOLESWORTH 2: Pass the marmalade and butter. Make it snappy.

MATER: ORTN'T NIGEL TO LEARN

DANCING? MY DERE?

PATER: How mush do it cost?

MOLESWORTH 2: Toste and more tea.

ME: After all entertanement at parties you can't beat throwing the old pink blancmange, mims, my swete.

MATER: O.K., rat you'll take dancing next term and like it.

That is the trubble with the youth of the world there is no justice, no court of appeal.

In the shabby finery of ye olde st. custard's dining room whose floor as usual is littered with old prune stones there were scenes of rolicking gaiety last nite. Under the capable auspises of mrs maplebeck gay youngsters from the skool sported to the capable measures of miss pringle, the skool musick mistress.

'Take yore partners for the foxtrot!' yell mrs maplebeck.

Imagine with wot joy molesworth 1, the dasher o the palais, see that he is to dance with his best frend peason.

'May i have the pleasure, o weedy worm?' he sa bowing.

peason respond with a low curtsey.

'O.k., thou giant rat!' he sa, with a modest blush

And so the dance begin and as the evening wea on the joy and xcitement mount to fever pitch a fotherington-tomas do a solo pas de deux with 9 m.p.h., 3000 c.c. jump which send him zooming into the honors board. Finally the skool piano blow up

HEIGH-HO for sir roger de coverly.

with mitey explosion sending up mushroom cloud of
fluff, caterpillers, cig cards ect.

So you see. You may as well put up with it becos
DANCING canot be avoided. Later on i am told
you will grow to like it so perhaps at the moment we
hav not enuff incentives. In the meantime
HEIGH-HO for sir roger de coverly tipp-toes and
don't forget to make a luvly arch.

A FEW ROOLS FOR XMAS

Gosh super xmas is here agane cheers cheers. Every
boy and weedy gurl must remember not only that

this is a time of rejoicing but that they must BEHAVE. Here are a few of the molesworth-peason rools for xmas which we hope you will all obay:

ROOL 1
Claus, santa, rekognition of.

Everybode kno even tinies that santa claus is yore . . . well, hem-hem. It is a chiz for the pore old felow, however, if you let him kno you kno. When he entereth the bedchamber laden with presents, snore deeply: when he drop the lot, stir uneasily as if there were fairies about (see p. pan) Do *not* sit up in bed and sa: 'A masterly performance, yore timing is superb, even olivier ect could not hav done better.' If you do this yore pater . . . hem-hem will burst out larffing, molesworth 2 will fire a red moon space roket and you will do a handspring off the end of the bed. This may get yore mater in a bate, season of good will tho it be. Better far to lie quite still as she bends over the sleping cherubs and hear her doting words: 'If only he hadn't got your family's revolting nose he mite be quite good-looking.'

ROOL 2
Claus, Santa in shop and rekognition of.

Everyone kno this dodge it is only to attrakt trade. Tiny gurls and wee boys are led by the hand chiz and their mummies sa 'Look at santa claus.' (n.b. wo are they expected to do, kick him?) The effect of being told to look at santa differ widely among the younger genneration – some weep bitterly, some put their finger in their mouths, others run away screaming and there are some, like molesworth 2, who sa: 'O.k. santa. Wot you got for me?' For elder children the direct approche is required e.g. zoom out of the house of the elves and conduct an interview like a t.v. reporter.

'Is that beard real? Is it cotonwool?'

'Y . . . y . . . yes.'

'Is it true there's only sawdust in that sack?'

'No.'

'You're sticking to that?'

'Sawdust and wood shavings.'

'Would you or would not sa there is an element of deception tantamount to fraud in your conduct? Are you satisfied and do you contend that you came to this toy department in a reindeer sledge? Wot are you going to do about it?'

Father xmas ushually hav a simple answer to this. e.g. i'm going to chase you round the elves house, into the wonderful gardens, through aladin's cave, and into the fairy grotto and if i get yer, mate, i'll do yer.' So beware.

ROOL 3
Dances, Fancy Dress, Corekt Deportment.

When told that dere mrs cracklby and dere lady fotheringay hav thort it a delicious idea to hav a fancy dress dance, most weedy gurls jump up and down in the air. 'Oh, mummy,' they sa, 'can i go as a pixie?' Boys are difrent. Being used to the horors of life at st. custards they take the dredful tidings with a stiff upper lip e.g. mater, nothing on earth will make me go. i uterly refuse. Comes the day, however, and there he is driven in the family tumbril, exposed to the jeers of the mob and why – he is dressed as a jester and smell of mothballs. Yore mater hav given you the famous words 'You will enjoy it once you get there' – and wot a mad delightful press of gay young people clad in multi-coloured costume greets the eye. Wate, however, until the eye getteth hit with a jelly bunged by little sally who hav come as tommy steel. WACKO! Lead me to the blancmange. Honor must be satisfied.

Gosh super xmas is here agane

ROOL 4
Wot to say when another boy's present is nicer than yores. Sa nothing. Just burst into tears and howl the place down.

ROOL 5
Parents, care and upkepe of, at xmas.

There would be no real xmas without parents. Therefore hem-hem it is as much their day as yores. There are several ways in which you can make it a true fragrant xmas for yore parents. Be sure to wake at 5.30 in the morning and trip down to their room to show yore presents. Paters get as much fun as the boys from tranes and cowboy pistols, altho the hour may be early. Then later do not forget to ask yore pater to mend the toys you hav broken and get him to share yore interests by making a vast dredger or cantilever bridge with yore bumpo construktion outfit. The really thortful will give him a nice elektric shok with their tiny toy crane. That will really make mums larff!

A BRITE FUTURE FOR YOUTH

DING-DONG-PIP-CLANG!
DING-DONG-PIP-CLANG!

Ye olde bells of ye olde church ring out merily – tower shake, rafters quake, death-watch beetles tremble in their shoes. Never hav there been such a din since molesworth 2 pla fairy bells on the olde organ

DING-DONG-PIP-CLANG!
DING-DONG-PIP-CLANG!

Ye olde bell-ringers drink more BEER and bells go

DONG-PIP-CLANG-DING!
PIP-PIP-PIP-PIP!

(n.b. wher hav DONG, CLANG and DING gone? They are lying flat on their backs like their extremely rude forefathers (peotry) and they wil feel terible tomorrow.)

What is all this about? It is the NEW YEAR Hooray, hooray, hooray! And the bells are ringing in until the appeal for £1000 to save the church from destruction zoom from its perch and strike ye olde vicar on his olde balde nut.

So once agane another year lie before us with all its brite promise. Everyone be he man woman or child (posh prose) will be wondering wot he can do to improve and, in come cases, it ought to take a whole year to find out. Take headmaster

GRIMES for xsample. Pikture him if you can on jan 1 writing his resolutions in his study while the candle gutter fitfully in the botle. This is wot he write:

RESOLUTIONS

Less food and all tuck forbiden . . . more dissipline . . . buy 60 new kanes . . . put up skool fees . . . borow up to £100 from new master before others can tell him . . . more produktivity in lat. fr. algy, geom ect . . . tune skool piano . . . more water in ink . . . new chromium plated counter for whelk stall . . . buy super new car . . . molesworth?????????

So, pleased with his work, he larff fritefully and creep through the cobweb passages of empty st. custards to his iron bed.

But not all are like GRIMES most want to do GOOD in the new year tho there is not much chance of it. Youth is brave, noble, fearless ect and face the problems of the age with brite, clear-eyed confidence. Even weedy gurls make resolutions chiz which are absolutely wringing wet e.g. you can imagine wot ermintrude (you kno the one with an ickle-pritty bow who dance a fairy dance at parties) write in her little lavender book.

RESOLUTIONS

Take more cowslips to miss pringle . . . improve my salt, mustard, pepper at skipping until i am as good as basil fotherington-tomas . . . press more leaves . . . make a chum of gloria . . . take more and more cowslips to miss

*pringle . . . kepe my back so strate i fall over backwards
. . . don't be nasty about jenifer's lipstick . . . kepe my
desk tidy . . . take millions of cowslips to miss pringle.*

And so it go on and even me, molesworth the
goriller of 3B, am not unmoved by the sentiments of
the season. Helping myself to 7 spoonfulls of sugar in
my tea at brekfast i look pensive.

'Tell me, bro, wot are you thinking, o weedy wet?'
sa molesworth 2, making a lake of treakle in his
poridge.

i slosh him and return to my reverie.

Time 2000.

*Scene: The laboratory of sir nigel molesworth, full of
atommic instruments, retorts, bunsen burners ect. A copy of a
horor comic lie on the table and, in the corner, a plektodo-
troscope revolve slowly, making calculations.*

*Enter molesworth 2, now grown more hideous than ever.
He is an interviewer for t.v.*

MOLESWORTH 2: Good evening, sir nigel. This
place does not half ponk, if i may sa so.

SIR NIGEL: Even with the technical progress of the
20th century no one hav been able to elliminate
ponks from labs. They used to be called 'stinks'
you kno hee-hee-hee.

MOLESWORTH 2: now, sir nigel, one of your
inventions was a cure for smoking, was it not, clot?

SIR NIGEL: Yes, yes, That was a simple matter. i
made a cig that was so long no one could reach to
the end to light it. A simple application of the laws
of pythagoras hee-hee-hee.

MOLESWORTH 2: How weedy. But yore greatest

'Ah yes, that removed the figgs from
syrup of figgs. A grate boon.'

invention, that by which you are world famou
was the droposcope?

SIR NIGEL: Ah yes, that removed the figgs from
syrup of figgs. A grate boon.

MOLESWORTH 2: No, clot, the droposcope.

SIR NIGEL: Ah yes, i'm sorry. A little hard of hearin
The droposcope. That was the first ballooon to g
downwards: i'm afrade it made nonsense of si
isaac newton and, of corse, the rusians wer
grately discomfited.

MOLESWORTH 2: Was not a boy called peason, a
old skool frend, associated with yore diskovery?

SIR NIGEL: Peason? Well, i did kno him and he di
a little of the elementary alg ... mind you, i don'
want to sa a word against him ... but you kno, o
quite the wrong line ... quite hee-hee-hee.

MOLESWORTH 2: Hav you anything else to sa, si
nigel, in the glory of your later years?

SIR NIGEL: Oui. Scram, you clot-faced worm, or
will utterly bash you up.

(*He seizeth the microphone and throweth it in the plektod*
troscope. A bird sing: a worm turn ect.)

And so it go on. But i do not think i will ever be th
BRANE of BRITAIN as every other boy will b
Perhaps by that time there will be room in the worl
for a huge lout with o branes. In which case i mi
still get a knighthood.

THE END

The Donkey Rustlers

GERALD DURRELL

This lively story with a Greek island setting tells h
Amanda and David plot to outwit the unpleasant lo
mayor and help their Greek friend, Yani. The village
and especially the mayor, depend on their donkeys
transport. If the children are to blackmail them successfu
the donkeys must disappear – and disappear they do,
the consternation of the whole village . . .

Told in Gerald Durrell's dashing style with his ov
particular brand of humour, this story will be eagerly re
by older children.

Ghostly Experiences

CHOSEN BY SUSAN DICKINSON

The remarkable revival of interest in ghost stories at the present time is curious, for ghost stories traditionally belong to that great age of story telling: the 19th century. And yet, despite the distractions of the television screen, ghost stories are much in demand particularly among the young. Here you will find examples of ghost stories ranging from R. L. Stevenson and J. S. LeFanu in the 19th century to the most contemporary of contemporary writers – Alan Garner and Joan Aiken.

Some of the stories are truly spine-chillers; some of the ghosts are gentle, some are not; but the collection should provide plenty of ghostly 'pleasure'.

'A splendid collection of supernatural adventures.'
New Statesman

'The stories in this collection have been chosen with discrimination and illustrated with a sure intuition.'
Growing Point

The New Noah

GERALD DURRELL

Boa-constrictors, paradoxical frogs, hoatzins, bush babies and tucotucos—they're all part of what Gerald Durrell casually calls his 'big family'. Each animal in his menagerie exhibits such curious habits and eccentricities. There was Cholmondely the chimpanzee, for example, who was 'king' of the collection, liked a good cigarette and his tea not too hot, but had a horror of snakes! Cuthbert the curassow loved to collapse across people's feet when they weren't looking.

Gerald Durrell describes not only the capture of these rare and exotic animals in Africa and South America, but also the problems of caging and feeding them. Footle, the moustached monkey, insisted on nose-diving into his milk, while the Kusimanses—nicknamed the Bandits—found Durrell's toes the most delectable thing in camp!

The Donkey Rustlers is also a Lion.

The Armada Lion
Book of Humorous Verse

CHOSEN BY RUTH PETRIE

Here's humorous verse from Edward Lear, Lewis Carroll, Hilaire Belloc, G. K. Chesterton, Kenneth Grahame, John Betjeman, Ted Hughes, Spike Milligan, Michael Flanders, Roy Fuller and many more.

Poets well-known and unknown offer humour and nonsense of every sort.

There's even '. . . a young man of Japan
Whose limericks never would scan;
  When they said it was so,
  He replied, "Yes I know,
But I always try to get as many
words into the last line as ever I possibly can".'

The Greatest Gresham

GILLIAN AVERY

The three Greshams were prim, correct Victoria
children, ruled by 'what other people might think
—but in their hearts they longed to be somethin
quite different. The two Holts *were* quite differen
and in the Greshams' eyes totally 'unsuitable'. The
read at the table, ate sweets between meals and swun
on their front gate!

But Richard decided to take the Greshams in han
for he felt they ought to develop 'an independer
mind'. And so 'The Society for the Achieving o
Greatness, Broadening of Horizons, Enlarging of Idea
and the Cultivating of Independent Minds' was borr

The rules were uncompromising—Amy had t
renounce her precious pink rabbit, Julia to trav
to Westminster Abbey in a railway carriage (but th
Greshams were forbidden to venture from their fron
door alone!), and poor Henry to climb the apple tree
All this in the name of 'Greatness'!